Vengeful
PRINCE

KIARA MORGAN

Vengeful Prince Copyright © 2022 by Kiara Morgan All rights reserved.

No part of this publication may be reproduced, stored or transmitted in any form or by any means, electronic, mechanical, photocopying, recording, scanning, or otherwise without written permission from the publisher. It is illegal to copy this book, post it to a website, or distribute it by any other means without permission, except for the use of brief quotations in a book review.

This novel is entirely a work of fiction. The names, characters and incidents portrayed in it are the work of the author's imagination. Any resemblance to actual persons, living or dead, events or localities is entirely coincidental.

Cover Design & Formatting: Acacia Heather, TheGraphicsDistrict

Chapter 1

LILY

The front doorbell rings and I already know it's Ronan Fitzgerald, the current leader of the Irish mafia in New York who has arrived.

When my papa told me I would marry a man almost 30 years older than me in less than 3 months, I felt my life crumble away into the depths of the darkest parts of the world.

I just turned 18 years old a few months ago and always knew as the daughter of Chicago's Italian mafia boss, Lorenzo Mancini, my marriage would be arranged.

I had assumed it would be with one of my papa's underbosses' sons or one that is still single. Not a man who's almost triple my age.

My mama said I was lucky I was marrying another mafia boss, as it would secure my place as Queen. But I have lived my entire life as Princess of Chicago and loathed the obligations and expectations that came with it.

To say I was sheltered would be an understatement. I barely went out unless it was for school or family obligations.

VENGEFUL PRINCE

I didn't have any friends since every girl and boy in my class knew who my family was and what they did.

At a point when I was child, I was so desperate for a connection with anyone that I began talking to someone online. When he asked to meet me at a McDonalds, I didn't see anything wrong with meeting a friend.

I snuck out of school and took a bus by myself for the first time. When a grown man who claimed to be a child online appeared in front me of, I was confused why my online friend lied about his age in that moment.

Luckily my papa's guards were able to track me down and find me before anything happened. They dealt with my "friend" by putting a bullet through his head.

When they brought me home, Mama called me stupid and naïve. I didn't understand why until years later.

I was always late to learn. It took me making mistakes to realize what I had done. I had no one to tell me otherwise or teach me. Aside from my brother Lorenzo Jr, or Enzo as he goes by, no one really paid attention to me.

I was just a mafia princess to be looked at but never touched or spoken to.

I hear a knock on my door and my mama pops her head into my room. "Lily, it's time to come downstairs and greet your future husband."

My stomach feels heavy at hearing the word husband. I had asked my older brother Enzo about Ronan as soon as Papa told me of the marriage arrangement. His pitied look was all I needed to know. I had heard rumors about him being maniacal before as well but didn't think much of it until now. Ronan was not a man to reckon with.

"Coming," I say to my mother who is busying looking up and down my body before giving me a pleasing smile.

"I'll be downstairs." She turns on her heels and leaves my room.

I straighten and look at myself one last time in the mirror. I had wanted to wear a more conservative dress, but Papa had insisted I wear something that would make me look more of an adult.

Now here I stand in a black mini dress that barely covers my ass and the top is low enough to emphasize my cleavage which I paired with the highest pair of heels I own.

For my makeup I tried to keep it simple to accentuate my emerald green eyes, and my long dark brown hair is curled in loose waves down my back.

I head towards the stairs to greet our guest and can already hear the chatter and laughter echoing through the halls.

With each step I take, my steps feel heavier. I feel as though I am walking to my execution and maybe I am.

I follow the voices to the living room and soon as I enter, the room becomes silent. I see my brother Enzo leaning against the far wall with a drink in his hand.

My papa raises to his feet and approaches me after doing a quick glance over my outfit. "This my daughter Lily."

I turn towards the person he is speaking to and find a tall middle-aged man with light brown hair mixed with some grey strands and blue eyes.

He is handsome for his age. Of course, his age is obvious with the wrinkles around his eyes and crease marks on his forehead.

That handsome face morphs into something lethal when he gives a shark-like smile. A tremor goes through my entire body at being under his gaze.

There is something frightening about him that tells my brain to run and don't ever stop.

"Lily, this is Ronan Fitzgerald," my papa says before nudging me forward.

I take heavy steps forward and stick out my hand. "It's a pleasure to meet you." My manners coming naturally despite the fear running throw my veins.

That is the one thing my mama said I was good at. Behaving. I did what I was told without a fight or argument. My previous nanny had said it had to do with my need to win people's love by pleasing them. It didn't work.

Ronan takes my slightly shaking hand into his rough callused hand and kisses the top gently. "The pleasure is all mine."

My mama raises to her feet and claps her hands together. "Let's have dinner. Our cook has prepared a beautiful meal for you Ronan. I'm sure you will enjoy it."

I can see the gleam of excitement in my mama's eyes. Mine on the other hand, I can already feel are empty.

The dinner went well, but I didn't miss the leery looks Ronan gave me throughout it. Every time he would look my way and give me that predatory smile, I wanted to crawl into a hole and hide.

After dinner, Ronan and my papa moved into his office to discuss business. Enzo joined them. Despite being only a few years older, my papa has started training him on taking over as the next Capo of the Mancini family.

My mama advised me to go upstairs and to stay in my room, but I couldn't help but hide near the stairs waiting for them to come out so I could hear something.

After what felt like ages, I hear my papa's office door creak open. I make sure to stay hidden behind the staircase which prevents me from having a good look from my spot.

I see Papa and Ronan whispering something before they shake hands and Papa opens the door for him to leave.

Once Ronan leaves and the door is shut, I quickly straighten and head towards my papa. "What did the two of you talk about?"

Papa frowns at my sudden appearance. "Did I not warn you previously about eavesdropping?"

I can tell he is angry, but I need to know if it involved me.

"Papa please," I plead.

"You should tell her now," I hear my brother's voice behind me.

I turn towards Enzo. "Tell me what?"

I fear what I am about to hear. From my brother's tone, it doesn't sound good.

Papa loosens his tie before addressing me, "You will be leaving tomorrow for New York." He says it with so little emotion that I think I must have heard wrong.

"Say that again? I thought the wedding wasn't for another 3 months," I ask in a daze.

"You heard me, Lily. You will leave for New York tomorrow morning. Ronan wants you close by before the wedding, but he knows of our customs and won't taint you before the wedding night."

Great, my virginity is protected for another 3 months.

"Why can't I stay home? I don't want to stay with him."

Papa's frown deepens. "You will be living with him for the rest your life once you're married. But it would ruin your reputation and mine if word spread that you and Ronan shared a home before the wedding. Which is why you will be staying in your own apartment for now. I will make all the arrangements."

I'm confused at having to move to New York so soon. "Why do I even need to leave? Wouldn't it be better for me to stay here at home?"

"The Irish are at war with the New York Italian family, the Vitales. He wants you nearby in case they find out about our alliance and try to approach us to sway us to their side. By sending you to New York now, we are assuring the Irish we stand by them and if we double cross them, they would have you."

I feel my throat going dry. "Have me?" As in if Papa double crosses Ronan, they would be able to kill me since I will be in their city.

Papa doesn't answer, and I turn to Enzo for help but he doesn't say a word. Even if he did, it wouldn't matter. My papa would do what he thinks is best for the organization. But the difference is I can see guilt in my brother's eyes unlike my papa's. They are throwing me to Ronan Fitzgerald like some toy he can either keep or smash into pieces.

Chapter 2

NICO

When our ally, the Russian mafia family the Petrovs told us Ronan had finalized his deal with the Mancini family, I was livid. The bastard went after my brother Alessio, the Capo of the Vitale Family. He tortured my sister-in law, Anna, and kidnapped my niece, Emma. I had made a vow to my brother I would bring Ronan to his knees and hand him over to Alessio to kill. I planned on keeping that promise. What I didn't expect was Lily Mancini to be in New York City so soon.

Nikolai Petrov used his connections within the government to find out that the Mancini family had created a fake identity for Lily and she was moving to New York before the wedding.

Despite my initial hesitations to form an alliance with the Petrovs, they have become good allies.

I watch from across the street as Lily Mancini exits the back of her town car. She turns and looks around at the tall buildings as if it's her first time seeing such tall buildings.

Her mesmerizing emerald eyes take in the view while the wind blows her chocolate brown hair to the side.

She gracefully pushes back her hair with her delicate hands and smiles at the driver before heading inside the building.

She almost reminds me of an angel. She doesn't know it, but I planned on dragging her to hell.

LILY

The view of New York City is amazing. Living in Chicago, I occasionally had gone downtown for parties and functions and always loved the city life.

But living in downtown was never an option for me. Papa would never allow it. Plus, Mama would always remind me I was too dumb and naïve to live alone. Maybe I was.

I was always told from a young age that my purpose in life was to marry a man my papa approved of and be a good wife. Anything else was not even an option. I was never allowed to make my own choices. Everything was always decided for me. It eventually made me into a shell.

Despite having to marry Ronan, I think I might like living here.

The town car stops in front of a tall building. The driver who picked me up from the airport under the alias Lily Williams gets out of the car and opens the door for me.

I take a step out and I'm in awe at the number of tall buildings. Some people would find the bustle and noise from the traffic to be annoying, but I love it. It makes me feel closer to others. As if I'm not alone.

I tilt my head up to try and get a better view of how tall the buildings are, but they look endless. The wind blows my hair in all direction, and I push it back.

"Here you are, miss." The driver takes out my suitcase from the trunk and puts it in front of me. I was only able to pack one bag as my papa informed me all the rest of my things will be shipped on a later date.

"Thank you." I grab hold of my suitcase and walk into the building of my new apartment.

I walk up to the concierge, a boy who is probably only a few years older than me.

He looks up from his computer screen and his eyes widen before giving me a smile. "Can I help you?"

"My name is Lily Williams, I was told I could get my apartment key here."

"Do you have a piece of ID, Miss Williams?"

I pull out the fake ID Papa gave me and slide it across the marble desk. "Here and you can call me Lily."

The concierge gives me boyish smile and pulls out a pair of keys from the desk drawer. "Here you go, Lily. And you can call me Matt."

I grab the keys from his hand. "Thank you, Matt."

As I turn around and head towards the elevators, I hear him say from behind, "Anytime!"

Once I get into the elevator, I head to the 15th floor where my apartment is located. I exit the elevator into a hallway and I find my door and unlock it.

As soon as I walk in, I'm amazed at the apartment.

My mama had told me it is a one bedroom apartment with disgust. You would think it was some shit in the hole place in a sketchy neighbourhood.

Instead it's a beautiful apartment with brick walls and dark wooden floors. When I first walk in, a small kitchen is to my left and next to it is a small dining room. After that there is a cozy living room with huge arched windows.

I walk down the small hallway and find two doors. One opens to a small bathroom and the next is my bedroom. Similar to the rest of the apartment, the room has brick walls, with one wall having giant windows similar to the living room. There is also a small bathroom and a tiny walk-in closet in my bedroom.

It's small compared to the one I have at home, but I love it none the less. It's perfect for me. I don't need anything large or fancy.

I can't help the smile that crosses my face at the thought of living here on my own. I was a bit worried being in a new city by myself without any guards, but Papa assured me with my identity, no one would even know who I am. He had used a government agency who made fake IDs for cops or witness protection members.

I can be a normal girl, living a normal life in the city for the next few months.

I decide to unpack and change my clothes to adventure out and explore the neighbourhood.

Considering it's late June, I change into a pair of denim shorts and a white tank top with lace detailing.

I'm looking through my suitcase for a hairbrush when I hear a knock on the door.

I halt and panic wondering who it could be. All of sudden the realization I really am alone hits me. The daughter of a dangerous mob boss out in the open for any one of his enemies to come and take.

Even though Papa had said the fake identity would protect me, they aren't one hundred precent foolproof. Even snitches in witness protection can be tracked down.

The knock gets louder. I tip toe towards the door and peak through the door peephole. My heart drops. It's Ronan.

I don't know why I am surprised to see him. He is my fiancé and I was informed by Papa he would stop by occasionally to keep an eye on me.

I had hoped considering his current situation with the Vitale Family and the secrecy of me being in the city, our interactions would be limited until the wedding.

I open the door hesitantly and he looks me up and down.

His pupils dilate in size and I get the urge to slam the door in his face and hide. But I know better.

He moves forward and I take a step back to put some distance between us. Ronan slams the door behind him as he makes his way in. My brain is telling me to run but I'm frozen on the spot.

He towers over me. "Do not ever keep me waiting." I don't respond fast enough and he grips my cheeks with one hand hard. "And answer me when I speak to you!" he seethes.

"Yes," I mumble out with his painful grip still piercing into my cheeks. He looks at me for a while, as if trying to find something wrong.

Finally, he lets my cheeks go and I quickly push myself against the wall furthest from him.

No one has ever touched me like that. I'm the Mancini princess. If anyone had dared put their hands on me, my papa would cut them off.

Not because he cared about me, but he would consider it an insult that someone dared touch something that belonged to him.

Ronan walks into the living room and takes a seat on the couch and motions with one finger for me to come. I know I should go but my feet refuse to move. They feel like bricks cemented into place.

"Don't make me come there, Lily," Ronan warns.

There is something startling scary in his tone that tells me not to anger him.

My feet finally listen and move as if they know to go into survival mode. Once I am near him, I stop about half a metre from him but he grabs me by my wrist and pulls me into his lap. My heart is racing against my ribcage and all my panic alarms are going off at once.

Ronan places his hand on my knee and then moves up my thigh. I try and jerk up but he grips my waist tightly.

"Don't move or I will punish you and you won't like it." His voice is laced with warning.

He continues his exploration by moving his hand up my stomach and when he cups my breast, I have to force myself to stay still.

"You're going to be a good little girl for the next three months," Ronan says.

I know he isn't asking but I still nod my head quickly.

"I will come by occasionally, but I expect you to be on your best behaviour when I am not around. Your father gave me permission to handle you as I see fit as long as you are not tainted before our wedding. Which is unfortunate, I could have had some fun with you."

My body goes stiff, but I try to stay calm.

Ronan gives me a smile that sends chills throughout my body. Suddenly, he gets up and I'm thrown to the floor. Ronan kicks me hard in my ribs, causing the air to be sucked out of me, making me wheeze.

"That is for keeping me waiting. Next time open the door when I first knock."

I am gasping for air while holding my side when he pushes his foot down on the spot he just kicked me in. "Remember what I told you Lily, be a good girl."

I give a haphazard nod and he laughs before making his way to the door. A few seconds later I hear the door open and then he is gone.

I pull my knees into myself and cry while lying on the ground.

Chapter 3

NICO

Ronan just arrived at Lily's apartment a few minutes ago and I consider calling in back up and taking him out here and now, but I need to be smart.

He is not alone. He has his entire security detail with him, and it will only cause a large shoot out in the middle of the street. There are risks of someone getting injured or us being seen.

Even with politicians and the police in our pockets, they would cause a fuss at the major media frenzy this would cause. They cover our backs on the condition we keep things contained and out of public view for a price.

Ten minutes after arriving Ronan exits the building, gets into his car and leaves with his security. I wonder what he and the little Chicago princess were doing? I will soon find out.

LILY

After crying for a few minutes, I give myself a pep talk and get off the floor.

It is dark when I look up. The sun has already set.

I would not let Ronan ruin my day. The day I marry Ronan will be a day worth crying over as my life will be over but until then I will live the next 3 months to my fullest.

Coming to New York early could be a blessing. At home I would have been locked away until my wedding day but at least here I can go out and do everything I have wanted to do. There is so much I have not done and wished I could see.

As I change my outfit to a pair of skinny jeans and off the shoulder black top, I decide to make a list of things I want to do before my wedding.

As I make my list, I can't help but feel sad. I have lived an isolated life and have not really lived.

My parents, they didn't really care about me, but they also restricted a lot of things. All they cared about was my brother, the heir to the Mancini family.

But I don't blame my brother. He is the only one who showed any interest in me.

Once I'm dressed and ready to go, I give myself another pep talk. Do everything and anything you want to. *I will have no regrets,* I tell myself over and over again.

I lock the door and throw my keys in my Chanel bag and head towards the elevator. I consider going back and changing my bag considering I am alone and don't want the unnecessary attention. Wearing an expensive designer brand would call in attention for sure.

But before I can head back, the elevator dings open, and I tell myself not to second guess myself.

Instead I flip the Chanel logo side inwards so no one can read the label. I tell myself I am just a normal girl.

Once I arrive on the ground floor, I give a little wave to the concierge Matt before heading out. He returns the wave with a smile and I make my way outside.

The cool summer air calms me as it hits my skin. The distant traffic noise makes me feel at ease.

I always hated the silence back home. I would play TV shows and movies in the background to end the silence.

I head down the street and look around the neighbourhood.

There are a number of cute shops that are now closed but make a mental note to visit tomorrow during the day.

I pass by a bar and the devil in me tells me to go in. The sane part tells me to walk on by and keep moving but I let the little devil sway me. *No regrets, remember?*

I open the bar door and I'm met with pumping music and chatter from other customers.

I head towards the bar and take a seat. I feel a bit of excitement at being somewhere I'm not supposed to be. I've never been to a bar or a club before. I decide this is another thing I can cross off my list.

The bartender walks over to me. "What can I get you, babe?"

My face reddens at him calling me a babe. I am about to ask for suggestions when a female waitress comes around and elbows the bartender in the back. "Don't forget to ask for her ID, dipshit."

"Ah, right. Can I see a piece of ID?"

"Sure," I respond to the bartender. I pull out my fake ID my papa gave me from my purse and hand it to the bartender. I know it says that I am 22 years old. I doubt Papa thought I would use this ID to get into bars when he gave it to me.

The bartender nods and hands it back to me. "So what can I get you?"

I put the fake ID back into my purse. "Vodka tonic."

I have never had it and have no idea if it's good but that's the only drink I can recall from the TV shows and movies I have watched.

The bartender makes quick work at making my drink and places it in front of me. "Let me know if you need anything else, babe." He gives me a crooked smile before turning around and walking to the next customer across the bar.

If I didn't think my face could go any redder, I was wrong. A simple smile and being called babe could make me blush. I bet my face looks like a beet right now. Usually, guys don't flirt with me considering my last name but here no one knows.

I take a sip of the drink and almost spit it out. It tastes like nail polish remover. Can't believe people drink this nasty stuff. I don't want to look like a prude so I decide to take small sips, each sip tasting worse than the previous. I feel like I might gag if I keep drinking.

I hear a low laugh behind me. "Not much of a drinker huh?" I turn towards the stranger's voice. I'm taken off guard when I see a tall, dark haired, and probably the most handsome man I have ever seen slide into the stool next to me.

I can feel my heart beating rapidly against my chest at the sudden appearance of this stranger.

My tongue feels heavy and I can't seem to form words. He motions for the bartender to come. "Can I get a whiskey on the rocks and one cosmopolitan?" The bartender nods, making the drink at unreal speed, and puts the drinks in front of the stranger that has somehow made me lose all ability to speak.

The handsome stranger slides the pink colored drink towards me. "Try this, I bet this drink will be more to your liking."

I want to refuse but my body seems to have a mind of its own. I pick up the pink colored drink and take a sip slowly, expecting it to taste like nail polish remover. To my surprise it's a tangy fruit taste.

"Wow, this is good," I say on autopilot. I'm surprised I was able to speak and consider maybe I imagined it.

The handsome stranger laughs. "I thought you would like it. My name is Nico." He holds out his hand for me to shake and I think about it for a second. I don't think Ronan would like me talking or interacting with other men.

But then I remember how much of an asshole he is, and he can't tell me what to do yet. Not for another 3 months at least.

I put my hand into Nico's much larger hand. He closes his hand around mine, caressing his thumb up and down my hand in a soothing motion.

A spark goes up my spine at his touch, but I try and stay focused.

"It's nice to meet you Nico. I'm Lily," I say, but it comes out breathy and quiet.

Nico gives me a smile, an unbelievably gorgeous smile. If I didn't think my heart could beat any faster, I was wrong.

Chapter 4

NICO

The little princess had left her apartment and wandered the streets of my city in a pair of jaw dropping tight denim pants that made every male that walked by turn around and stare at her ass.

To top it off, the little princess had no idea the effect she had on men. Or on me.

When she walked into a bar, I saw this as my chance. I could snatch her up and take her. Call Ronan and gloat the same way he did when he took my sister-in-law, Anna.

But when I walked into that bar and saw Lily sitting at the bar drinking, I couldn't help myself. I needed to get closer to her. Not to take or harm her but just get close to her.

There is something hypnotising about her. I'm not sure if it's her striking emerald green eyes, her perfect body, or the way she so innocently lives unaware of her surroundings. Maybe it's a combination of all three.

When she took a sip of her alcoholic drink and scrunched her little perfectly straight nose in disgust, I couldn't help but laugh at how cute she looked.

It's clearly her first time drinking and a vodka tonic was too strong for her. I ordered a more appropriate drink for her and her emerald eyes shined in excitement when she took the first sip. I could see little specks of darker green mixed with her emerald eyes light up like fireworks.

Every time she reacts, the specks of green change to a different shade of green.

"I thought you would like it. My name is Nico," I say out loud and hold out my hand for her. She shyly slides her small delicate hand into my much bigger and hardened hand, and I can't help but feel up the softness in her hands.

Everything about her is soft and delicate.

After a few seconds, she clears her throat and pulls her hand out of mine. "So, Nico do you live around here?"

"No, I have business in the area." Business as in you.

"What kind of business?"

I know she is just trying to have conversation but telling her I'm in the mob might make her run.

Despite her family being part of the business, she is technically the enemy, and I can't have her finding that out right now.

"Sales." I keep it vague and hope she doesn't ask any more questions.

She nods. "That's nice."

"What about you?" I change the topic from me to her.

"I just moved here from Chicago." She freezes and I see the panic in her eyes. Probably at the fact she has said too much.

I take a sip of my whiskey. "What was the reason for the move?" Giving her an out from her sudden panic.

She shrugs clearly unsure of her story. "I've always wanted to live in the city. I guess this is my one chance."

My phone vibrates and I take a look at the screen. It's my younger brother Carter. I send the call straight to voicemail. I will deal with him later.

"Well, I'd be happy to show you around. The city is quite large and can be a very dangerous place for a woman." Especially when the enemy is sitting right beside you.

She hesitates. "I don't think that's a good idea."

"Why not?" I lean in towards her causing her breath to hitch. "Come on, it'll be fun." Fun for me at least.

She bites on her plump pink lower lip before quietly answering, "Okay."

I instantly smile at her agreement. "What's your number?" I ask.

Again, she nibbles on her lower lip. Clearly having second thoughts but I see her phone laying on the counter in front of her and swipe it up before she changes her mind.

"What are you doing?" she asks.

I type in my number in her phone and send a missed call to myself to have her number saved on mine. "Saving my number on your phone." I hand the phone back to her and get up from my seat. "I'll message you tomorrow."

I drop a hundred dollar bill for the drinks and I start walking away when I hear her shout from behind me, "What? Wait!" I turn back around and give her a wave and walk out of the bar.

Once I'm outside, I head towards my car parked in the alleyway across the street and dial Carter's number.

He picks up after one ring. "Why did you decline my call?"

"Because I was busy."

For a moment there's silence before he speaks. "Did you capture Lily Mancini?"

"Not yet, but I will soon."

LILY

The handsome stranger's name is Nico. It matched him perfectly. For the first time I felt I was on fire all throughout my body and didn't know how to extinguish it. I can tell he is more experienced and knows what he is doing. I was completely out of my element, but I didn't care. I wanted to know more about him.

I was always told fires tend to be unpredictable and can severely burn you. In that moment I was willing to get burned.

My mama would say that is the dumb in me. Maybe it was.

He said he would message me tomorrow, but I don't know what that means.

When he volunteered to show me around the city, I knew it was a bad idea. I have never been alone with a boy before let alone a man who wasn't a hired guard of my papa's.

Nico's charming smile and dangerous handsome looks made me forget about common sense.

I told myself in the beginning of the night that I would live as much as possible before my wedding to Ronan. Having a bit of fun couldn't hurt, could it?

After I finish my drink, I take out my wallet ready to pay for my drink. Even though Nico's one hundred dollar bill could have covered both our tabs, I pay for my own drink anyways.

I get up from the bar stool and feel a little lightheaded from the alcohol, but I steady myself on the counter and push myself off to head out.

Once I am outside, I walk the same path I took earlier towards my apartment.

Luckily it is less than a five-minute walk to my apartment because the alcohol is taking its toll. I can feel myself feeling sluggish and my legs feel like they are made of jello.

As soon as I reach my apartment building, I quickly enter and don't bother to wave at the concierge. I just want to get into bed and pass out.

The day has been long from my move from Chicago to New York

to dealing with Ronan. At least it ended well, I tell myself with a smile.

Maybe it's just the alcohol making things better.

I take the elevator to my floor and fumble my keys out of my bag. For some reason I drop my keys twice before I was finally able to open the door.

Once I'm safely inside I head straight to my bedroom and toss my shoes and purse to the side and climb into bed. The room begins to spin like a ride until I close my eyes and fall asleep.

I'm woken to an overly bright sunny day. It hurts to open my eyes so I squint until I can adjust to the light.

I'm definitely a light weight considering it only took two drinks for me to feel like I was on a tilt awhirl ride at the carnival. I didn't even finish my first drink since it made me want to gag every time I took a sip.

I groan and stretch out my body when I hear my phone ring. The noise is alarmingly loud and I get the urge to throw it at the wall. I lazily grab my phone from the nightstand and see it's my papa calling.

I instantly pick up the call. "Papa?"

I had planned on calling him yesterday when I arrived to let him know I got here safe but then the anger of him marrying me off to Ronan prevented me from doing so.

"I hear you haven't been behaving."

I get up into a sitting position in my bed. "What do you mean?"

Does he know I went out to a bar and had a drink? He couldn't have. I'm alone here without any guards with me. I bite on my lower lip thinking I've been caught already.

"Ronan called. He said he came by to see how you were and you were rude to him." My papa's voice rises with anger. "This is not how I raised you!"

I want to say you didn't raise me. Even Mama didn't even raise me.

I was raised by a number of nannies or was left alone in a room to entertain myself. That was my childhood. Waking up to some new woman claiming to be my nanny only to be let go a few weeks later.

"Papa," I start, "I was not rude to him at all. In fact, he hurt me." For some reason I expect Papa to side with me and be angry on my behalf that not only did Ronan hurt me, but he also physically laid his hands on me.

"I was too easy on you and now you embarrass me. You will behave and if you don't then I can't blame Ronan for finding ways to teach you, can I?"

My eyes sting from pain. "Papa..." How could he care so little about me? Do I mean so little to him? I may have not been born as a boy but I am still his daughter.

"Enough, I will not say this again. Behave and do not ruin this alliance. I have too much riding on this and I won't have you destroy it," he warns.

The worst my papa or mama have ever done is take away my toys when I was younger but to think they would be okay with Ronan hitting me hurts.

I want to argue and plead with Papa but I know it's pointless. He probably won't even blame Ronan if he beats me to death at this point.

My mouth feels dry but I force myself to speak. "Don't worry, I will behave, Papa."

"Good, I will call again in a couple days after I get an update from Ronan." After saying goodbye, he hangs up. Call *after* he gets an update from Ronan not before.

Part of me thinks I should take this chance and run.

Living on my own doesn't sound as bad as marrying Ronan but Papa would find me. You can't run from the mafia. I had never thought Papa would kill me but if I embarrass him by breaking this alliance, he just might from his tone.

Enzo might try to protect me, but he is not Capo yet and holds no power within the organization.

My phone pings, but this time it's a message. I'm thinking it's from papa reminding me of our conversation but to my surprise Nico's name flashes across the screen.

I hover my thumb over his name, trying to decide if I should open it or not. My stomach feels like there's a hundred butterflies inside just from seeing his name on my phone. Finally, I force myself to press his name and open the message.

I'll pick you up tonight for dinner. What's your address?

My breath stills at the thought of seeing him again today. This would be my first date. I tell myself to stop over thinking this, he might just want to take me out to dinner as friends. I saw on shows and movies people do that sometimes.

I type in my address and hit send without thinking. Maybe that wasn't a smart idea. Giving a stranger I just met at a bar my address doesn't sound like a bright idea. I get a response a few seconds later.

I'll be at your place at 7pm to pick you up.

There is no going back now. Part of me doesn't want to.

I look at the clock, it's almost noon. I decide I have a few hours to figure out what I am going to wear. It might not be a date, but it is still my first and I'm not going to waste it.

Chapter 5

NICO

I sent the little princess a message informing her of the time I will be picking her up. The plan was not to dine her before kidnapping her but there is something about her.

What could it hurt to have some fun before I ruin her life?

My phone rings; this time it's my older brother Alessio.

He is currently in Italy with his wife and children.

I answer after the second ring. "How is the vacation going?"

"Some vacation. I still have to work even in Italy. Not to mention how hard it is to control our businesses from the other side of the world."

"It's only for a few weeks. Were you able to meet with the Morellis?" The Morelli Family owns the largest and most advanced weapons manufacturing company in the world. They have built their empire on the blood of their enemies. We have been trying for years to forge a deal with them, but they have refused each time.

"No, I was told they are no longer in Italy. How are things going with Ronan? I hear Lily Mancini arrived in New York yesterday."

"She has."

"And yet you still haven't made the move to take her."

"I plan to, but I thought I could get close to her and find out what she knows about Ronan before I take her." My desire to get close to Lily is for other reasons but Alessio doesn't need to know that.

Alessio is silent for a few seconds. "Nico, if you are having second thoughts, we can get Ronan another way. I don't like using some girl as a pawn anyways."

"No, Lily is our best shot. If there was another way, we would have done it by now. Eye for an eye." The thought of hurting Lily strangely doesn't sit well. She's an innocent but she is part of our world.

When Ronan kills one of our men, we repay him back by killing two of his. Lily being a woman shouldn't matter. After what Ronan did to Alessio's wife and child, it only seems fair we do the same to him.

For years women and children were off limits, but many crime families have crossed that line by targeting the wives and children of high-ranking members. Alessio's first wife was killed by the Yakuza, which we eradicated them from the entire east coast for.

I hear a wailing cry from a baby from Alessio's end. Alessio sighs. "Daniele is up, I need to go. Keep me updated."

"Will do." We end the call there. I have some last-minute work I need to finish before I meet the little princess.

LILY

I spend the entire day planning my outfit but somehow time just flew by. Thankfully my boxes full of clothes arrived from Chicago this afternoon so I had more selection to choose from.

I have changed my outfit 10 times already. I've tried on a casual outfit with jeans, basic top and sneakers to a full tight dress with high heels.

I realized halfway through doing my makeup Nico never mentioned where we are going.

What if takes me to the park and I am dressed in a ballgown or to some fancy restaurant and I'm dressed in sneakers and denim shorts?

After trying every piece of clothing I own, I settle on something in between. A white spaghetti strap dress with strappy high heels. Simple enough for the park but formal enough for an elegant restaurant.

I look at the clock and I have 5 minutes before it is 7. I quickly run around my room grabbing my purse and tossing my lipstick and anything else I might need in there. My phone rings and I see it's a text from Nico.

I'm downstairs.

I get giddy all of a sudden like a 14-year-old about to have her first kiss. Sad and pathetic me might as well be 14 since I haven't even had my first kiss before.

I quickly text Nico saying I'm coming.

I run to the bathroom and do a quick look at myself. My makeup is flawless, and my hair is in soft waves. Once I am satisfied with my appearance, I head downstairs.

Once I get out the elevator, Matt from the reception desk at the lobby gives me a wave and a smile. I wave back to him and make my way out.

Once I get outside, I see Nico leaning against a black Lamborghini with his legs crossed at the ankles while texting on his phone.

My breath is sucked right out of me at seeing him. He looks like perfection.

He looks up and gives me that dangerously handsome smile and tucks his phone into his suit pants. "Lily, you look beautiful."

I can feel my face going hot at the compliment. "Thanks."

He opens the door of his car for me, and I take a step towards it to get in when a thought crosses my mind.

Nico is probably still in his 30s. How does someone this young afford a half million dollar car? The people I know who can afford luxury items like this don't make their money the legal way.

"Is something wrong?" he asks.

I turn towards Nico. "What did you say you do again?"

"Sales." Sales. That could mean anything.

He must see the question in my eyes and continues, "My family owns a number of profitable businesses."

"Ah, so you inherited all this." I motion towards the car.

He chuckles. "Yeah, but I also work hard for it."

Now I feel stupid and completely embarrassed. "I'm sorry, I didn't mean to offend you. Usually people aren't able to afford cars like this at your age."

"It's okay. Get in."

I smile and finally get into the car. Thankfully he didn't take offense to my question.

But the thought doesn't leave me. I look around the car to see if I notice anything out of the ordinary. But I'm not sure what I am looking for. No criminal is going to leave their stash of drugs or guns sitting in the back seat of their car.

Nico gets into the driver side of the car. "Ready to go?"

I give him a short nod and he starts the car and puts it in to motion. I tell myself to stop overthinking things.

For all I know, Nico is some rich stockbroker's son or inherited a multi millon dollar cattle farm from his grandparents. Not everyone is a criminal or part of the mob.

"So where are we going?" I ask trying to fill my mind with other thoughts.

"There is a restaurant near Central Park that has the best steak."

I turn in excitement and squeal unladylike, "I've always wanted to go to Central Park!"

Nico laughs. "We can go there after."

Realising I probably sound like some crazy tourist, I try and bring my excitement down.

"Is there anything else you want to see?" Nico asks.

I lick my lips and bite on my lower lip trying to think of some other places I want to see. I had made a list before coming to New York and after what happened with Ronan, I don't want to take anything for granted.

I turn to Nico and notice him staring at my lips. I release my lower lip and clear my throat. "Um, I've always wanted to see Times Square, the Brooklyn Bridge, and the Empire State Building."

Nico nods and turns back to face the front. "We can visit those places tomorrow and maybe a few others. Or we can space them out on different days if it's too exhausting to do all in one day."

I'm left speechless. A few minutes ago, I was worried I offended him, putting an end to whatever this is, but here Nico is planning the next couple of days.

I smile at the thought of our next outing. "I would love that."

Nico pulls up in front of a restaurant called Sapori and the valet comes to open my door.

I step out and Nico comes around and puts his hand on my lower back. I shiver at his touch as he guides me towards the restaurant entrance.

We enter a beautiful and elegant restaurant. There are a number of people waiting for their tables, but Nico continues to the front passing the waiting crowd.

A woman with dark hair and a black dress looks up and smiles. "Hello, table for two?"

"Yes," Nico says.

The woman nods. "We have been expecting you. We have made all the arrangements as requested. Please follow me." I'm curious what arrangements Nico has made. I didn't think he would put so much effort into tonight.

We follow the woman through the restaurant all the way to the back. She opens a door at the end of a hallway and motions for us to enter.

VENGEFUL PRINCE

We are led into a private room with only one table. There is a large chandelier hanging above the table with a small fireplace to the side. Considering it is summer, the fireplace is not turned on, but it would be a great place to come during the winter.

Nico holds out the chair for me and I take my seat at the table, while Nico takes one across from me.

The dark-haired woman hands us the menus. "The waiter will arrive shortly to take your orders, Mr. V-I mean sir." The woman gives an uneasy smile towards Nico before backing away and making an exit in a rush. You would think the building is on fire considering how quickly she ran out of here.

"That was odd," I say to Nico.

Nico shrugs. "I make women nervous." That I believe. He has made me second guess everything I have said and done since we met.

I look over the menu unsure of what to order. "You said the steak here is good right?"

Nico nods. "If you're unsure, I can order something I think you would like for you?"

"Considering you were right about the drink from the bar, I think that's probably a good idea." I laugh.

Nico looks at me weirdly and I wonder if I have something on my face.

The waiter walks into the room. "Are you ready to order?"

Nico places an order for the both of us along with a bottle of wine. I tell myself to not drink too much considering how easily I got drunk yesterday. I don't need to be embarrassing myself in front of Nico.

A few minutes later the waiter returns with the bottle of wine and pours two glasses before placing the bottle to the side near the table.

I take a sip of the wine and I'm surprised at the fruity taste. Nico seems to know exactly what I would like. He seems to know me better then I know myself.

Nico's phone rings and he pulls it out from his pocket with a frown. "I'll be right back. Just need to take this call." I nod as he gets up and heads towards the door.

Chapter 6

NICO

I walk out of the private room and make my way down the hallway until I find a secluded spot.

I look at my phone and see it's my wife Gia calling. That crazy bitch is a thorn to my side. The only reason I married her is because she lied and said she was pregnant. Since our wedding, she has made it her mission to make my life a living hell. But the dumb bitch didn't realise I would make her regret ever messing with me. Every time she did something stupid, I made her pay tenfold.

I pick up the call. "What?"

"Is that any way to talk to your wife?"

I roll my eyes. "What do you want?"

"It's my friend's birthday tomorrow and I need a new dress."

"And?"

"And you took away my cards remember!" she screams into the phone.

I smirk. "You caused that yourself. You went after Anna and now you are paying the consequences." The dumb bitch went after Alessio's wife a few months ago. Alessio had me cut her off financially to teach her a lesson.

Somehow, she has found ways to still get money. I suspect she has been selling her designer bags or going to her father for money. He is only a soldier so he can't afford the lifestyle Gia seems to think she is entitled to.

"How long am I going to be cut off for? I need money for things!" she screeches on the other end of the phone.

"Take it up with Alessio." I hang up the call before I have to listen and hear her whine some more.

Even if Alessio forgives her for her behaviour with Anna, I have no plans on reinstating her credit cards. I am enjoying her struggle way too much.

Just as I'm about to head back to Lily, I see the waitress from earlier who showed us to our private table. She almost blew my cover.

The restaurant is one of many that belong to the Vitale family. I picked this place because of the exclusive private table away from prying eyes.

I had made it clear to the staff that no one was to call me by my last name and no one part of the organization who knows me should be allowed in tonight. But of course, a simple task was too hard for her. I make a mental note to deal with her later.

I make my way to the private room and find Lily crouched in front of the fireplace.

"The weather is too hot for the fireplace," I say.

Lily turns to face me. "I was just thinking this would be a great place to have dinner during the winter."

"We can come back here in the winter if you want." A lie I tell her. She won't be here when winter rolls around. Not after what my family and I have planned for her.

She gives a sad smile before straightening to stand up. "Maybe." She must know herself that she won't be around when winter comes.

Unlike me, she thinks she is going be married and living with Ronan by then. But he won't be alive once we are done with him.

The waiter walks in with our food but stops when he sees us standing near the fireplace. "I'm sorry. Are you not ready yet?"

"No, we're ready." I motion for the waiter to go ahead and place the food down.

The waiter places our food on the table and heads back out. I place my hand on Lily's lower back and she shivers under my touch. She did that earlier too and I like the reaction she has to my touch. I guide her back to the table and she takes her seat.

Her emerald eyes light up at seeing the food in front of her. She purses her lips as she grabs her fork and knife. She gently slices the steak with her delicate hands.

Lily takes a bite of the steak and smiles. "You were right, the steak here is amazing."

I smile at her reaction. She is filled with such innocence. "I'm glad you like it."

The rest of dinner goes smoothly. Lily tells me a list of other places she wants to see here in New York. She seemed to enjoy not only the steak but the wine as well. She's only had 3 glasses, but I can tell it's taking its toll on her.

I pay the bill and we head out of the restaurant. Again, she shivers at my touch as I guide her out. I'm tempted to find out what her reaction would be if I touched her in other more sensitive spots.

Once we are outside, Lily turns into me and grips my arm. "Can we take a walk in Central Park for a few minutes?" She points across the street towards the park.

I can't help but say yes to her when she looks at me with her enticing, beautiful eyes. "Sure, if that's what you want to do."

We walk across the street towards the park and Lily smiles in excitement. She places her arm around mine as she looks up at the night sky. Her porcelain skin glows under the setting sun, a stark contrast to her chocolate brown hair that falls down her back.

When she walked out in that white mini dress and heels, I was thrown off and forgot who she was for a second.

She is breathtakingly beautiful.

I'm not the only one who's noticed. Every man that walks by ogles her and every woman who passes by envies her.

Lily doesn't even realise how stunning she is. She is always very naïve about her surroundings.

She walked the streets of New York alone in the dark yesterday without a care in the world. After I had hung up my call with Carter, I waited for her to leave the bar to make sure she got home safe.

Anyone could have taken her or even worse. She has clearly lived a sheltered life. You would think as the daughter of a Capo she would be taught to be more cautious of the dangers around her.

After a few minutes of walking, Lily turns towards me. "Thank you for taking me out." She looks at me with such innocent and pure eyes. All the while I am planning her ruin.

"Well, I plan on doing it again."

"I'm sure you have better things to do then take me out." She warmly smiles.

There is something about her smile that is contagious, and my mouth turns up to mirror hers. "I will make time if I have to. We should head back soon, it's getting late."

She pouts in the cutest way. "Fine, but only if you promise to bring me back here again."

"Promise," I say without thinking. I want to shoot myself for making such a promise. A promise I might not be able to keep.

Lily sways on her feet. "Okay, let's go."

We head back towards my car, and I drive her back to her apartment. When we arrive in front of her building, I get out and open the door for her.

Once she is out, she gives me another one of those innocent smiles. "Well I guess this is goodnight."

She turns around and heads toward her apartment building door.

I know I should just let her go. She is Ronan's soon to be wife. But logic seems to have been tossed out the window when I grab Lily's wrist.

She turns around and faces me with confusion. I pull her towards me and wrap my arm around her back and lean down and kiss her.

She freezes at my touch and doesn't kiss me back at first but then places her hand on my cheek and deepens the kiss. Her warmth is pressed against me and I can't help but want to take it further.

My judgment finally makes its way back to me and I pull away from her. Lily looks up at me with those gentle eyes of hers that make me feel like an asshole for playing with her emotions.

I clear my throat. "Goodnight, Lily."

She smiles. "Goodnight," she says before she turns and heads into the building.

I know that was stupid and reckless but all I can think about is the cold feeling on my cheek where Lily's hand was only a few moments ago.

Chapter 7

LILY

Last night was the best day of my life. I felt free and relaxed. I didn't have to worry about what people were going to think or say.

I wasn't the Chicago princess but just a normal girl on a date. But what I loved most is how Nico treated me. Like a normal person.

Boys in Chicago always kept a distance from me. But Nico isn't a boy.

When he kissed me, I felt I was on some sort of high. The butterflies in my stomach were soaring in every direction.

His presence alone makes me nervous and on fire. I keep wanting to get closer to him and feel him even if it's for a short while.

I stretch in my bed as I look at the clock. It's 9 in the morning. The sun is bright and shining through my curtains.

I lean over to my bedside table and grab my phone. No messages or calls.

For some reason I can't help but feel disappointed. I know it's still early in the day, but I had expected Nico to contact me after last night.

His lack of interest hurts more than my parents ever could. From them I expect coldness and indifference, but I was sure with Nico we had a connection.

I consider texting Nico but then think against it. I don't want to sound desperate or needy. Besides, I shouldn't cling onto something that won't last. After all I'm engaged to someone else. No matter how good it felt.

I get out of bed and decide to start unpacking my remaining boxes shipped from Chicago.

After doing my morning routine of washing my face and brushing my teeth, I put my hair in a ponytail and make my way to the living room.

The boxes full of stuff are taking up half the room. I can't help but sigh at having to unpack everything. I didn't realize how many pieces of clothing I had until now.

After unboxing about 3 boxes and piling my clothes to the side, I hear my phone ring. I drop everything and run to grab it. My stomach drops when I see it's a message from Ronan instead of Nico.

I will be dropping by tonight. Do not keep me waiting.

My hand involuntarily goes to my side where he kicked me last time he was here. I can already sense the threat behind the message.

I had hoped Nico would contact me for a second date, but I guess tonight is not the right time anyways. I toss the phone onto my couch and continue with my task of unpacking to keep my mind off tonight.

NICO

I walk into our family-owned club Encore and make my way upstairs to Alessio's office that I am currently using while he is away.

Since it's daytime, the club is completely empty besides the few staff members cleaning up from the previous night.

Once I enter the office, my younger brother Carter is sitting on a chair in front of the desk waiting.

"What are you doing here? Weren't you meeting with some suppliers today?" I ask.

Since Alessio is not here, Carter and I have split his duties between the two of us.

Carter was supposed to meet with a few weapons suppliers for more guns and ammo. I had hoped Alessio would have closed the deal with the Morellis giving us better and more powerful weapons but that seemed to have failed.

Carter rises to his feet. "I was, until I got a call from one of the captains who said he saw you with some hot brunette at Sapori's last night."

Not sure what I am more annoyed about: someone calling Lily hot or snitching on me to my younger brother.

"And?"

"Please tell me it's some random girl you're fucking and not the Mancini girl."

I try to restrain my anger. "And what if it was Lily Mancini?"

Carter crosses his arms over his chest. "This was not the plan."

"No, the plan was to kidnap some innocent girl and torture her."

"Not some innocent girl but Ronan Fitzgerald's fiancé. Same girl that also happens to be Lorenzo Mancini's daughter. Plus, we weren't going to torture her. Just use her as leverage against Ronan."

"Whatever." I wave Carter off and head towards the desk and take a seat behind it.

We may not have planned to physically torture Lily but kidnapping and keeping her hostage can be considered a mental form of torture.

Not sure when I decided I was against this plan. Especially considering it was my plan to begin with. It was supposed to be an easy grab and attack Ronan. Now it's turned into something entirely different, all because I wanted to get closer to her.

"Lily Mancini is all we have against Ronan right now," Carter reminds me.

"I know," I snap.

Carter raises one of his eyebrows at my reaction. "So, the plan is still on?"

"Yes," I seethe. "For now, have a trusted soldier keep an eye on Lily. Once we get the right opportunity, we will take her." I hate the feeling I get in the pit of my stomach, but I need to remember who she is. The enemy.

Carter nods but I can tell he wants to say more. "Fine."

"Also make sure that the captain who saw me and Lily keeps his mouth shut."

"Already done. I need to get going, I have work to do."

Carter walks out of the office leaving me alone with my thoughts.

I shouldn't have kissed Lily last night. And now I can't stop thinking about it or her.

I considered calling her this morning but forced myself to stop. I can't be forming any sort of attachment to her. She is the enemy and means to an end only.

Nothing more I tell myself. Now I just need to keep saying it until I finally believe it.

Chapter 8

LILY

I have cleaned up the entire apartment from floor to ceiling. After unpacking and organizing my closet, I kept staring at my phone waiting for it to ring.

I decided I needed to keep myself busy and cleaning was all I could think of.

It is 6 in the evening when I hear a knock on the door. I know it's Ronan but a small part of me hopes it might be Nico. He never did call or text me.

He promised he would take me to the park again and he would show me around. Maybe he changed his mind after last night.

I walk over to the door quickly and open the door. Ronan looks unimpressed as he glares down at me. I want to wither away under his terrifying gaze.

I move to the side to let him in and see a young man with dark hair and brown eyes standing behind him. Probably one of his bodyguards. He stays outside as Ronan makes his way in.

I close the door behind us and follow behind him as he makes his way to the living room. He looks around the room, analyzing every detail. Almost trying to find something wrong or a fault.

"Is something wrong?" I ask.

He turns and faces me. "Has anyone been here?"

"No," I say quickly.

"This place looks different."

"I cleaned this morning."

Ronan takes a step forward and I get the urge to step back but don't move. I know it's pointless as he could easily grab me, and it would probably only piss him off. And that's the last thing I want to do. I may not be the sharpest, but I learn with each mistake I make.

He puts a finger under my chin and tilts my head up. "If I find out you're lying, I will beat you bloody."

A tremor runs down my spine at his threat.

He smirks at my reaction to his threat. "Don't worry, I will make sure no important part of you is permanently damaged."

I can feel my heart beating all the way up to my ears. I take a hesitant swallow before responding, "I'm not lying." My voice comes out in almost of a whisper. As if it can't get any louder out of fear.

He lets my chin go. "Good. What's for dinner?"

"Dinner?" No one said anything about dinner. He mentioned coming over in his message but never that he wanted me to make him dinner.

Ronan frowns. "Don't tell me you didn't prepare anything for your soon to be husband? I came all the way here to see you and you couldn't bother to prepare a meal for me?" His face shows no emotion, but I know that is only a mask.

"I can quickly prepare something now," I scramble out. I'm not sure what I can, considering I haven't gone grocery shopping and have been getting my breakfast from the café down the street or ordering take out for lunch.

Ronan tsks. "What did I tell you about making me wait? You want me to wait while you cook some half assed last-minute dinner?"

He takes another step forward, but this time I can see the fury in his eyes. I know right then from his look I'm doomed.

I quickly spin on my feet and run towards the door. I don't think, I just run and try and get as far away as possible.

As soon as I reach the door and go for the doorknob, I feel Ronan grab my hair and I am being yanked back.

Ronan pulls me by my hair and drags me back to the living room. "Now I have to teach you a lesson. I warned you and yet you still don't listen."

He lets go of my hair and I drop to my knees. "Please, I won't make this mistake again," I beg.

I've never begged in my life, but I can feel it in my bones that he is not above killing me. I just need him to overlook this once and I will learn. I always learn and don't make the same mistake again. Always.

Ronan smiles down at me. "If I let this go, you will never learn."

"I promise I will learn. I might make mistakes but after the first I won't make it again. I swear it." My voice comes out panicked and quick.

Ronan shakes his head. "Another thing I don't like besides waiting is repeating myself. I will not repeat myself again. I will not let this go and your pathetic begging won't do anything either."

"Please," I try again but before I can even get a word out a punch in the face knocks me to the ground. The room is spinning and I feel lightheaded but before I can even think to move, Ronan kicks me in the stomach. It's still sensitive from his last kick there.

I cry out in pain but it's useless as Ronan grabs me by my hair and forces me to face him. "Next time I won't be so gentle," he warns.

If this is gentle, I don't want to know what he will do when he is actually pissed off.

He lets my hair go and I fall to his feet pathetically.

"I guess we can go out for dinner," Ronan says with indifference.

I raise my head up in shock towards him. He is not really thinking of going out to dinner with me looking like this. "You have 10 minutes to get dressed and ready." He looks at his watch on his wrist. "Time is ticking, Lily."

I quickly push to my feet and run to my room without thinking. I have 10 minutes and can't be late by a second. I don't want to know what he will do if I'm late getting dressed.

I head towards my closet and panic at what outfit I should wear. If I'm underdressed, he might beat me and if I'm overdressed, he might beat me again. Same problem I had last night but instead of excitement, I feel fear.

I'm tempted to go back into the living and ask where we are going but I know I don't have time for that.

I pick out a pair of skinny jeans and a white blouse. I run to the bathroom to change and lock the door behind me. As if the door will protect me from Ronan.

When I turn to the mirror, I can't help the tears that fall one after the other down my cheek. I look like a mess. My hair looks like a nest and my right eye and cheek is bruised from Ronan's one punch. I gently touch the bruised area and cry silently at my situation. How could my family do this to me?

"Five minutes!" I hear Ronan shout from the living room.

I quickly remove my top and see my entire right side is bruised from Ronan's kick.

More tears come out, but I don't let that slow me down. I need to get changed and be out in less than 5 minutes.

I fix up my hair and change into the white blouse and jeans. I head back to my room and grab the strappy heels I wore last night with Nico.

What a difference a night can make. I went from having the best day of my life to the worst.

I consider going back into the bathroom and applying a bunch of makeup to cover my bruises but I'm running out of time. Besides, no amount of makeup could cover the bloody mess my face is right now in the short amount of time I have.

I head back into the living room. Ronan looks up at me and then looks at his watch.

Ronan frowns and with annoyed tone says, "Ten seconds to spare. Lucky you."

He wanted me to fail! The sick bastard enjoys torturing me.

More tears fall down my cheek despite my attempt to hold them in. Ronan pushes to his feet and walks over to me. He touches my cheek and wipes my tear with his index finger causing me to flinch at his touch.

He smiles at my reaction. "Don't tell me I've broken you already. Where is the fun in that?" I glare up at him, but he just smiles at my pain. "Let's go." He puts a hand on my lower back and I go rigid. I want to pull away from his touch. He doesn't seem to care as he guides me towards the door.

We walk out into the hallway where his guard is standing waiting. He looks at my face and then looks away.

Looks away from my bruised and bloody face.

The guard hits the elevator button. "Where to, boss?"

"I'm thinking Josie's Strip Club."

Strip club? He can't possibly be thinking of taking me there. Why would he want to take me to place like that? My breathing gets heavy at the thought of what Ronan could be planning.

Ronan leans down and whispers into my ear. "Don't worry, I just want you to learn some tricks. As my wife, you need to learn how to please me."

I can't believe that Ronan wants me to learn from strippers.

The elevator doors open, and Ronan pulls me in with him and his guard follows behind.

Ronan turns to his guard. "Carlo, make sure they have Daisy ready tonight. I like how she moves."

The guard named Carlo nods and takes out his phone and begins texting something. I look over at the guard again and can't help but think he looks Italian.

Ronan once again leans down and says into my ear. "Look at other men like that again and I might just be forced to rip your beautiful little eyes out from your sockets."

I begin to tremble with Ronan's hold still on me.

I don't doubt for a second he would blind me. I face the ground and remind myself multiple times of Ronan's rules as the elevator descends to the ground floor.

Don't make him wait. Don't make him repeat. Don't look at other men.

The last one is going to be the hardest considering half the population is male.

Once we reach the ground floor and exit the elevator, I keep my face down. Not only not to make eye contact with other men but I'm also too embarrassed and ashamed of my battered face and pathetic life to let anyone see me.

We reach outside and Ronan nudges me into a black SUV. He gets in after me and once he is settled, he motions for the driver to drive.

I keep my face down and stare at my hands in my lap the entire ride. After what feels like an eternity, we pull up in front of a sleezy building with neon lights and signs.

One of Ronan's guards opens the door for him, and he gets out. He puts his hand out for me to take but I hesitate. I can see his jaw tick at my hesitation, and I quickly grab his hand before he beats me in front of everyone to see in the open.

He helps me out of the SUV and puts his arm around my waist as we walk into the sleezy club.

The music is loud and pumping through the entire room.

There is a small stage in the middle of the club with a pole and a naked woman is spinning on it. I look down in embarrassment at seeing all her private parts on full display.

A greasy haired man guides us to a private area in the dark room. I don't get a good look at him since I'm trying my best to avoid looking at men directly.

Ronan pushes me down into the booth and sits next to me. The greasy haired man and Ronan say a few things but I'm too stunned to realize what they are saying or what is happening.

A few seconds later, drinks are brought to our table. Ronan hands me a glass and I again hesitate to take it.

Ronan sighs. "I guess I need to teach you a few more lessons." I instantly grab the drink with shaking hands. I don't need to be taught any more lessons.

A woman with bleach blonde hair and enormous fake boobs in a daisy duke outfit comes to our table.

She leans down, making one of her large fake boobs pop out of her low top. "Ronan, I have been waiting for you," she purrs. "What can I do for you?"

Ronan grins. "Daisy, I need you to show my fiancé how to suck a man's balls properly."

My eyes widen in shock at what I hope I misheard. Daisy moves herself in between Ronan's thighs and starts to unbuckle his belt.

My heart is racing a million miles per second. I need to get the hell out of here.

I move over in the booth to get away when Ronan grabs my wrist. "Watch carefully, Lily. If you can't learn to suck my balls properly, I might not have any use for your mouth."

I begin to tremble again and the ice in the drink in my hand chatters with each shake from my body.

Daisy finishes unbuckling Ronan's belt and pulls out his cock. She leans down and licks the tip. I look away but Ronan grabs my hair forcing me to look.

Daisy continues to lick and suck Ronan's dick while massaging his balls.

After a few minutes Ronan's body goes tense and his hold in my hair tightens painfully. I can feel pieces of my hair being ripped from my skull.

Ronan comes and Daisy licks it all up while having the biggest smile on her face.

Ronan finally lets go of my hair and Daisy finishes sucking with a pop. She gives Ronan a seductive smile. "How was that?"

Ronan leans back in the booth ."Good but next time Lily will do the sucking while you give instructions."

Tears fall down my cheek and I quickly wipe it away.

Daisy gets up. "Of course. I will make sure to give detailed instructions."

Ronan motions for his guard Carlo who is standing to the side. Carlo comes to the booth and hands Daisy a few hundred bills.

Daisy gives Ronan one last smile before walking away while shaking her ass.

Ronan puts his dick back in his pants. "What should we eat?"

I turn my teary face to him but don't know how to respond. I have zero appetite for anything right now. I want to go home and beg my parents to save me.

Ronan just smirks at seeing me like this. To him I am nothing but a punching bag and a whore.

NICO

I'm working on some business reports at Encore when my phone rings. It's Carter. I pick it up on the first ring.

"The soldier watching Lily has an update," Carter says.

This gets my full attention. I've been avoiding dealing with her all day but somehow my mind kept going back to her. "What kind of update?"

"Ronan came to visit Lily today but he was with half a dozen guards, so we couldn't go after him without causing a scene."

No surprise there. He has been heavily protected since our war began. Which is why it's been so hard to get to him. "Any other news?"

"Apparently Ronan took Lily to Josie's strip club."

"That sleezy dump on the north side of the city?" Why the hell would Ronan take Lily to a place like that?

"Yeah, and according to the soldier even though he had to keep a distance, he could see Ronan had his hands all over Lily." My blood begins to boil at the thought of that son of a bitch having his hands on Lily. "But the most shocking part was Carlo was there. He's one of Ronan's guards now." That little fucker. Carlo betrayed my family before running away like the rat he is. We have been searching for him for months.

"Anything else?" I say with clenched teeth.

"No."

"Okay, keep me updated. I have something I need to take care." I hang up the phone before Carter can say anything else. I grab my keys and head out.

If Lily thinks she can play housewife with Ronan and be all friendly to Carlo the rat, she has another thing coming.

Chapter 9

LILY

Ronan dropped me back at my apartment after having dinner at some restaurant across the street from the strip club.

The staff and the customers at the restaurant were all staring at me with pitying looks but no one said a word.

I just sat there while pushing my food around the plate. I didn't really have the appetite to eat anything after being beaten and degraded by Ronan tonight.

Ronan walked me to my apartment with his hand around me. I was scared to death thinking he was going to come in but thankfully he left as soon as I walked into my apartment. Of course, he made sure to remind me to be a good girl.

I have changed into a pair of pink silk tank and sleep shorts. My face looks like 10 different shades of purple.

My eyes sting with pain but no tears come out. It seems my eyes have dried itself out from all the crying.

I go through a box of things I didn't have to time unpack in the closet for my first aid kit I saw earlier.

After some digging, I finally find it and place the first aid kit on the kitchen counter.

I've just pull out some ointment when I hear a knock on my door.

My body starts to tremble at the thought that Ronan has returned. I run to the door remembering he does not like to wait. It's scary how easily my body reacts to a simple knock.

I pull the door open quickly and my body instantly relaxes in relief. It's Nico.

Nico looks at me with widen eyes. "What the fuck!"

At first, I'm confused at his reaction and then remember my face. I quickly place a hand over my right cheek and part of my eye in embarrassment.

He pulls my hand away. "What happened?"

"I just fell, nothing serious," I lie.

He narrows his eyes at me. "Just fell?"

"Yeah, just fell," I repeat.

His gaze is almost piercing. As if he can see through me and read my mind and soul.

I give a very bad fake laugh. "It's really nothing."

"Nothing?" His voice is calm but for some reason sounds deadly.

I try and change the topic. "What are you doing here?"

He doesn't say anything at first, only looks at me face. "I wanted to see how you were doing after last night and hoped we could hang out again. Can I come in?"

I realize we are still standing at my door. "Of course, come in." I move to the side and allow him entrance but then regret it right away. If Ronan found out, he would kill me. He threatened to beat me bloody for just suspecting I had someone over.

Nico walks into my apartment and looks around, like Ronan. Instead of how Ronan was trying to find a fault, Nico is just taking it in.

His eyes land on the first aid kit on the counter in the kitchen. He picks up the ointment. "Here, sit." He motions with his chin towards the kitchen stool next to the counter.

"I can do it myself." I try and grab the ointment from Nico's hand, but he raises his arm above his head.

He is obviously much taller than me which puts the container out of my reach.

"Real mature," I mumble under my breath.

He gives me a smile. "Sit."

I take a seat on the stool. Nico gently pushes my hair away from my face causing me to shiver from his slight touch.

He starts to dab the ointment on my cheek and eye area. Every time he touches me, I can't help the tingle that runs down my spine. I hate that he has this effect on me.

"There, now it won't leave a mark on that beautiful face of yours," Nico says.

I feel my face going red.

"So," I start.

Nico gives me that incredibly handsome smile of his. "So?"

I'm not sure what I'm supposed to say or do. I start to bite on my lower lip out of habit.

Nico zones in on my lips and his pupils increase in size causing me to freeze. He gently traces my lower lip with his thumb, sending a spark down my body all the way to my toes. "You need to stop that."

I let my lower lip go. "Sorry." Not sure what I'm apologizing for. I clear my throat. "It's too late to go out and I don't really have anything here for us to do."

I don't even have groceries. I'm not exactly sure why he came here so late. It couldn't be because he was hoping I would sleep with him. Even if I wasn't bruised up, I wouldn't sleep with a guy after one date. Even if he had a way of making the room spin whenever he is around.

Nico looks around the room and stops when he sees the television. "We can watch a movie or something."

"Just watch a movie. Nothing else?"

Nico gives a devilish smile. "Why? Were you hoping we could do something else?"

My face feels like it's burning hot. "No," I say quickly. "Just making sure you weren't here for any other reason. I'm not that type of girl."

"I know." He walks over to the couch and takes a seat before grabbing the remote to turn the television on. I slide off the kitchen stool and make my way to the couch.

The couch is a two-seater, but I take a seat closest to the edge possible.

I'm not giving him any ideas. I look at him from the corner of my eye and he turns to me and gives me a heart fluttering wink. Dammit. Why did he have to be so good looking and kind?

NICO

I had come to Lily's apartment in anger. She let Ronan touch her and not to mention she was hanging out with Carlo the traitor.

Which I know is unreasonable since Ronan is her fiancé and she is nothing to me. And Carlo was there as Ronan's guard.

But the illogical part of my brain refused to let this go. I was fuming all the way to Lily's.

I could feel myself ready to explode like a ticking bomb while I knocked on her door.

But as soon as she opened the door with her beautiful angelic face bruised up, my anger evaporated. Only to come back in full force at Ronan daring to hurt Lily.

She lied and said she fell but I can tell the difference in bruises from an intentional and unintentional hit. Ronan did that to Lily.

She is sitting next to me on the couch but is all the way at the end. The little princess thinks she can keep a distance from me.

I flip through the channels to find something good we can watch. I didn't come here to watch a show with Lily, but I had to come up with a quick excuse.

As I'm flipping through the channels Lily straightens. "Oh wait, the movie The Notebook is on. Go back."

I've never watched The Notebook but have heard of it. It's some sappy romance movie. I land on a boxing match. "Or we can watch this."

Lily scrunches her nose in the cute way she always does. "Come on." She leans forward and grabs the remote from my hand. "It won't be so bad. I promise."

Usually, I have quicker reflexes and could have prevented her from taking the remote but when she leaned forward all I could think about is the thin silk camisole she is wearing.

Lily smiles as she goes back to The Notebook. She crosses her legs on the couch. "Next time we can watch what you want."

"I plan on holding you to that," I say.

Lily turns to me and starts to nibble on her lower lip. Every time she does that, I have the urge to suck her lower lip. She stops nibbling when she notices me staring at her and turns her focus back towards the television.

Halfway through the movie, Lily falls asleep. Which is not a surprise considering how boring the movie is. It's nothing like reality.

She slumps to the side, and I catch her and gently place her head on my lap.

I trace her eyebrows, perfectly straight nose and those damn lips of hers that she won't stop teasing me with.

My phone rings and Lily moves at the sudden sound of my phone. I quickly pick up the call in an attempt not to wake her.

"Nico how are things going?" my brother Alessio says on the other end.

"Fine," I say just above a whisper. I don't want to interrupt Lily's sleep.

"Why are you whispering?"

"I'm not," again I say in a quiet voice.

Alessio's quiet. "I don't think I want to know what you're up to. How are things with Ronan going?"

I look down at Lily. "Okay."

"I heard Carlo is back in town and working under Ronan."

"He is."

"If you get him before I get back, keep him alive." I can hear the anger in Alessio's voice despite him trying to sound calm.

I smile at the thought of what Alessio has planned for Carlo. "Of course."

"If nothing else, I will call again tomorrow." And with that, Alessio ends the call.

I made a promise to my brother. And I plan on keeping it. Even if it means hurting Lily.

Chapter 10

LILY

I groan awake and look around at my surroundings. I'm in my bed in my room. I can't seem to remember how I got here. I turn to my left and find Nico sleeping next to me. I jolt up in panic.

What is he doing here? The last thing I remember is watching The Notebook.

I must have fallen asleep. But that doesn't explain how I'm in bed with Nico.

I look down and thankfully I am still wearing my clothes. Nico on the other hand is naked from the chest up at least. I don't want to know about his bottom half.

I look around the room and find his clothes tossed on the chair in the corner.

I gently poke Nico to try and wake him up. He doesn't move. I poke again but harder. Again, he doesn't move. I ball my hand into a fist ready to come down on his shoulder as hard as I can when he grabs my wrist at lightning speed.

Nico opens one eye. "That's not very nice."

I try and pull my wrist free from him, but he yanks me forward towards him. I land face first on his chest.

I feel his body vibrate underneath me as he laughs. I on the other hand do not find this amusing at all. My heart is thundering in my chest and my face feels hot to the touch.

I place my hand on his chest to pull myself up and glare up at him. "Why are we in bed together?"

"You fell asleep, and it was late, so I just decided spend the night here," he says with such nonchalance.

"That doesn't explain you in my bed. You could have slept on the floor."

"Why would I sleep on the floor when there is a perfectly fine spot in the bed right here?"

"My bed."

Nico smirks. "Are you afraid something might happen between the two of us?"

I widen my eyes in shock at his suggestion and quickly rip away from him and out of the bed. "No more sleeping in my bed."

Nico gets into a sitting position. "Okay, then what should we do if not sleep in the bed?"

If I thought my eyes couldn't get wider, I was wrong. I point my finger at him. "None of that either!"

Nico laughs and raises his hand in surrender. "Calm down, I was just kidding. So, what should we have for breakfast?"

"Breakfast?"

Nico swings his legs out of bed. "Do you want to eat in or go out?"

When did we decide we would be having breakfast together? What is going on?

I am just about to tell him I'm not interested in having breakfast when my stomach growls. Nico smiles at me. "I guess we can eat out since it would be faster."

Nico gets out of bed and I notice he is wearing nothing but boxers!

Nico stretches before saying, "I'm going to take a quick shower if that's okay." I don't say anything as I'm completely lost for words. He takes my silence as agreement and walks into the bathroom.

As soon as the door locks, I go into panic mode. If Ronan finds out, I'm good as dead. I shouldn't have even let Nico in last night.

Nico comes out of the shower a few minutes later with only a towel wrapped around his waist. He is all bronze and muscle. My mouth waters at the thought of touching his six pack.

I can feel my face warming up as I continue to gawk. "I need to get ready," I stumble out. I run past Nico and into the bathroom.

Once I have locked the door, I slump against it. What am I doing? I am clearly out of my mind.

I look up at the mirror and see my face. The bruising has turned to a gruesome purple. This will be my life in 3 months' time. Ronan gets his joy at torturing me. He is going to find one way or another to hurt me. In the meantime, if I could have some fun and live for once before I'm trapped in a marriage with him, why the hell not?

Remember no regrets.

NICO

I'm waiting for Lily in her living room when I get a call from Gia. I send it straight to voicemail. I have no idea what she wants but I know it won't be good.

She probably wants me to re-activate her cards again. Her guard had informed me she has been visiting her father multiple times a week. But he can only give her so much money. He can't afford to bank roll Gia's ridiculous spending habits. The only reason I put up with it is because I had hoped she would leave me the hell alone.

I send another one of her calls to voicemail.

I hear the door to Lily's room open and she walks out. She is wearing denim shorts and a white crop top tank that shows a sliver of her perfect flat stomach with heels. She seems to have covered the bruises on her face with makeup but if you look close enough you can still see them. They looked worse than yesterday.

I would love to punch Ronan in the face until it caves in.

She shifts between her feet. "Are you ready to go?"

I get up from the couch and give her a smile. "Yeah, let's go."

Lily grabs the keys and walks towards the door. Once we exit, she locks it behind us and throws her keys in her purse. We get into the elevator and head downstairs.

I can tell something is on her mind but don't ask. I don't need her running away from me by having second thoughts. I've been shutting my own thoughts down at how bad of an idea this is already. I don't need her telling me hers as well.

Once we exit the elevator, she waves to a guy at the desk in the lobby. He smiles and waves back to her.

"Who the fuck is he?" I ask in annoyance.

Lily turns to me. "That's Matt. He's the concierge." It annoys me even more that she knows the little punk's name.

Once we are outside, Lily points down the street. "There is a cute bistro a few minutes that way."

I shake my head. "No, I know a better place. I'll drive." I grab hold of Lily's hand and pull her towards my car. At first, I can feel some resistance but eventually she follows my lead.

Once we get to my car, I open the passenger side door for her. She walks past me to get into the car and the wind blows her hair in my direction.

Her hair smells like an intoxicating scent of strawberry. Sweet like Lily. I close the door behind her and make my way to the driver's side.

Once I get in, I start up the car and put it in motion. "So, I was thinking we could go to one of those places you wanted to see on your list."

Lily spins in her seat towards me in excitement. "Really? Where should we go? Maybe we can go to Times Square or the Empire State

Building."

I can't help but smile at her excitement. "We can go to both if you want."

She clasps her hands together. "Really?" As if she can't believe we can go to two places in the same day.

I nod. "Yeah but first let's grab breakfast."

Lily settles back into her seat, but I can see the radiance in her emerald eyes shine in pleasure. After a few minutes of driving, we make it to a small restaurant I've been to a few times.

It's not associated with the mafia but is a hidden gem within the city. After the dinner fiasco I realized it's best to take Lily to a restaurant that isn't owned by my family. At least here no one will know who we are.

I get out and walk around to help Lily out.

We walk into the restaurant and are greeted by a young man. "Table for two?"

"Yes," I say.

He gives Lily a smile. "Follow me." I want to kick the little bastard from behind as we are shown to our table.

He hands us the menus. "Is there anything else I can get you?" The little bastard is staring only at Lily while asking.

"No," I growl at him.

The bastard flinches before finally looking my way. "The waiter will be right with you to take your orders." He walks away in a hurry back to his spot at the front of the restaurant.

"This is a cute restaurant," Lily says as she looks around at the décor. "We should come here again."

"No, we will not."

Lily looks at me with confusion. "Why not? I thought you liked this place since you brought me here."

"I changed my mind."

Lily tilts her head to the side, trying to figure me out. Good luck with that because I can't even figure myself out these days.

She sighs. "Well let's still eat here because I think it's cute and I'm hungry."

The waiter comes to our table and takes our order.

"I'm just going to go the ladies' room really quick." Lily gets up from her chair to go to the washroom. As she gets up, her top raises up a bit higher. On her right side there are some ghastly looking bruises. As Lily is walking by the table towards the washrooms, I grab a hold of her wrist.

She halts at my sudden hold of her. "Is something wrong?"

Using my free hand, I pull up a bit of her top more giving me better view of the bruises. Fuck! They are worse than I thought.

Lily pushes my hand away from her, "I fell on my side too." Her voice is unconvincing as she gives me a small smile. The smile is forced while her eyes are full of pain.

I let go of her wrist. "You should be careful," I say in the calmest voice I can muster up. She nods before continuing on her way to the washroom.

I on the other hand think of a million different ways I plan on cutting Ronan Fitzgerald up. I had promised Alessio he can kill Ronan, but I can help torture the little fucker for a couple days at least.

When Lily returns, she slides into her seat and smiles at me. One look at those green eyes of hers and I can feel myself getting more entangled in this mess I created.

LILY

I could tell Nico was upset about something at the restaurant but once I returned from the ladies' room, he seemed to be over whatever was bothering him.

He saw the bruises from Ronan's kick on my side. I think he might have bought the lie about me falling but I can't be sure.

After having breakfast, Nico took me to a couple tourist attractions in the city.

Throughout the day I could feel myself getting more comfortable with Nico.

Every time he would touch me, it still felt like a spark igniting within me. He seems to have a way of doing that to me.

First, we went to the Empire State building. The view was amazing, but it was super crowded with all the other tourists around. Nico had pointed out he has a better view at his penthouse. When I asked him to take me there one day, he quickly said it was currently under construction. For some reason it sounded like a lie but I don't know why he would lie about something like that.

After that we went to Times Square. It was filled with hordes of tourists as well.

A man selling roses had offered me a free one as a gift. Before I could take it, Nico shoved the rose back at the poor man telling him no thanks. Nico claimed the seller was trying to trick me but I'm not sure how he could have tricked me with a rose. The man had nothing to gain by offering me a free flower; in fact he had more to lose since he wouldn't have gained any profit.

By the time we were done for the day, it was getting late. Nico grabbed pizza for us to eat back at my place while we watched a boxing match. It's only fair since I had said we could watch what he wants next time.

We're sitting on the couch eating pizza when my phone rings. I go into a panic wondering who's calling me. I pray it's not Ronan. I place the pizza on my plate on top of the coffee table. "I'll be right back."

I walk over to the counter where my phone is and see it is my brother Enzo. I walk into my bedroom and close the door behind me.

"Hello?" I answer.

"Lily, it's good to hear your voice."

I smile. "Yeah same here. Is everything okay?" My brother is the only one in my family who has ever actually cared about me. We don't get to spend much time together since my papa has been raising him to be the next Capo, but he has always made sure to check up on me. I think he feels guilty no one ever cared about me.

"Everything is fine. I heard Ronan had called Papa and told him you behaved last night when he saw you."

My insides twist and turn at the memories of last night.

"Enzo." My voice breaks as soon as I say my brother's name.

"What's wrong?" I can hear the panic in my brother's voice.

"I don't want to marry Ronan. He is a monster. You don't know how he is."

There is silence for a few seconds that I start to wonder if I might have lost the connection.

"Lily, I need you to listen to me. Papa will be retiring soon. It is only 2 or 3 more years and then I will take over. Once I am Capo, I will bring you back home. You just need to survive until I take over." Truth is I don't know if I can survive that long. But I know Enzo can't do anything as long as Papa is in power. "Lily, did you hear me?"

"Yeah, I heard you."

"Hang in there, Lily. I need to go now. But don't forget what I told you. I will get you out of there. I promise."

"Okay, call me again when you have time."

"I will."

Once the line goes dead, my heart feels heavy. There is no getting out of this marriage. I will have to marry Ronan but at least it will only be for a couple years and then Enzo will come for me. Enzo has never lied to me. If he says he is going to do something, he does it.

I head back outside to the living room and Nico looks up at me. "Is everything alright?"

"Yeah." I toss my phone back on the counter and sit next to Nico on the couch. The heavy weight of my future still presses against my insides.

Nico grabs my hand into his. "Are you sure? You can tell me if something is wrong."

Feeling his hand in mine seems to thaw away the pain and put it on the back burner. I smile at Nico. "Everything is fine." For now, anyways.

He nods and turns back to the boxing match without letting go of my hand. Almost like an anchor keeping me from drowning in my emotions.

In that moment he doesn't feel real. Someone like him can't be here in my apartment. Someone who wants to know how I feel, who cares to do what I want to do, and makes me actually feel wanted.

It's as if I've dreamed up some illusion.

I lean forward towards him and he turns to face me in confusion. He raises an eyebrow in a questioning look.

But I need to feel him and know he is real. I place my hand on his cheek and feel his stubble on the palm of my hand. Not only is he real but a warmth spreads down my body.

I'm mere inches from his face when he pulls me into his lap. "Don't test me, Lily," he breathes.

What he doesn't know is I'm testing myself. I lean up towards him and kiss him.

He pulls me further up his lap and now I'm straddling him as I kiss him deeper. I feel like I'm on a high. I bite Nico's lower lip and he growls against me. I can taste a tinge of blood from my bite when I feel something poking me near my inner thigh.

That's when I realize it's his erection. My heart is thumping against my ribcage, and my mind is swirling in circles.

I push away from Nico, finally coming to my senses. "We can't do this." He doesn't say anything but the look on his face tells me agrees for some reason.

Nico turns off the boxing match. "It's getting late. We should probably go to sleep."

"You're staying the night again?"

Nico smirks. "Might as well."

I hesitate for a second. Nico the spending the night here does not sound like a good idea but part of me doesn't want to be alone. I feel safe and protected when he is here. The pain is locked away and my concerns don't exist when I'm around him. The selfish part of me doesn't want him to leave either.

"Fine, but," I motion between the two of us, "nothing is happening between us."

Nico smiles. "Don't worry. I won't touch."

For some reason I don't believe him, but it is getting late and I'm tired. I untangle myself off him and head towards my bedroom and feel Nico following behind me.

Once I get into my room, I pull out my sleepwear and head towards the bathroom to change.

When I come out, I'm thrown off balance at seeing Nico laying with legs crossed at the ankles in my bed in nothing but boxers.

"You can't sleep like that!" I point towards him.

"Why not? I didn't bring a change of clothes. Does this bother you?" he asks in an almost challenging tone.

"No." I walk over to the bed and grab one of the pillows and shove it in between us.

He chuckles. "Come on Lily, you're overreacting."

I crawl into bed. "You just stay on your side of the bed and I'll stay on mine." I turn off the light and try and go to sleep. But all I can think about is the half-naked gorgeous man lying across from me. Eventually I'm finally able to drift to sleep.

NICO

The little princess tried to build a wall figuratively and literally between us.

When she kissed me earlier, if she didn't stop, I don't think I could have.

I can't help but wonder if she is saving herself for that fucker Ronan. He doesn't deserve her.

I toss the pillow wall she made to the side. I plan on breaking down all her walls one brick at a time.

I trace her long dark eyelashes. They look like half-moons against her porcelain skin.

She squirms in her sleep, and I take the opportunity to pull and shift her towards me. Her head is now on my chest and her small delicate body is pressed against mine.

Lily has engraved herself into not only in my life but into my heart and soul.

I know I should walk away while I can. But I'm a selfish man and I want Lily. She will one day hate me for this, but I can't let her go. She is mine.

Chapter 11

LILY

I wake up to an amazing smell. I open my eyes and look around my room. Nico is nowhere to be seen. I stretch and walk out into the living area and find Nico making pancakes in the kitchen.

"Where did you get that?" I know my fridge and cabinets are completely empty. I haven't had the time to go out and grocery shop.

"I woke up early this morning and bought some things from the market down the street." He places a pancake on a plate and pushes the plate in my direction. "Sit and eat."

I walk over to the counter and take a seat on the kitchen counter stool. No one has cared to ever cook for me. The house staff at home has but that's different. They're paid to cook for my family.

The one time I was ill as a child, I had asked my mom to make me chicken noodle soup and she told me to go ask the staff. In reality I just wanted someone from my family to care about me while I was sick.

Nico pours syrup on my pancakes and hands me a fork and knife. My heart feels heavy at the thought this is the first time someone has cooked me something not out of obligation.

Nico grabs a plate of pancakes for himself and takes a seat next to me and starts eating away.

I on the other hand try and take small bites in between telling myself not to cry and became an emotional mess.

After we are done eating, I get up to put the plates in the sink when someone knocks on the door.

My body stills. Oh no, what if that's Ronan.

Nico heads towards the door to open it and I drop the plates in the sink and run behind him to stop him.

Nico swings the door open and to my surprise it's not Ronan. It's a large bulked up man. He looks like he could squash me like a bug with his bare hands. He hands Nico a bag and nods before walking away.

"Who is that?" I ask.

"That's Mario. He works for my family. He was just dropping off some clothes for me to change into." Nico shuts the door and walks back towards the bedroom. "I'll be right out."

As Nico takes a shower, I finish washing the plates.

After a few minutes Nico walks out in a freshly changed suit. "I need to go to work but I'll be back tonight." He walks over to me and pulls me towards him and kisses me. I melt at his touch until he pulls away.

He smiles and pulls out my keys from his pant pocket. "I borrowed your keys when I went out to buy groceries. Also, I made a copy for myself."

He tosses my keys on the counter and gives me another peck on my lips before he walks out of my apartment.

I'm still in a daze until I realize he just said he made a copy of my key. I can't believe he made a copy of my key!

I'm not exactly mad he has a key to my place. But I need to talk to Nico the next time I see him. I can't have him coming to my place without warning. Especially if Ronan is here.

NICO

I'm at Encore working on financial reports when Carter walks into the office. I can tell from his grim expression he has something to say, and I already know what he plans on saying.

Carter takes a seat in front of the desk. "Where were you last night? You didn't come home." As in Carter's penthouse.

Since my marriage to Gia hit rock bottom, I've been staying at Carter's place since. He always nags me about crashing at his place, but I know he secretly likes having me there.

A few years ago, his girlfriend went missing and he went to a dark place. He has since come back from there, but he hasn't been the same since.

Originally, I had started staying there to keep an eye on Carter to make sure he didn't do anything while alone with his dark thoughts. But over time it became my place of escape from Gia.

"I stayed at Lily's," I answer Carter.

He doesn't say anything or show any emotion.

"Don't pretend like you didn't know. I'm sure the soldier you have keeping an eye on Lily informed you of everything."

"Then you don't need me to tell you how bad of an idea this. Playing with her emotions…"

"I'm not playing with her emotions," I interrupt Carter with more bite in my tone then I would have liked.

Carter looks me in the eyes and tries to read me. "Nico, this is bad."

"I know." I don't need to be reminded.

My phone rings and I groan at seeing Alessio's name flash across the screen. I hate that I already have one brother riding my ass, now I'm about to have two.

I answer the phone and put it on speaker before tossing on the desk.

"Is everything alright?" Alessio asks.

There is silence between me and Carter.

"Nico?"

"I'm at the office at Encore with Carter. I have you on speaker," I finally respond to Alessio.

"Then someone want to tell me what the fuck is going on?" Alessio's sounds impatient.

I know Carter is trying to protect me, but this is my mess. "I've been seeing Lily Mancini," I fess up.

"Seeing?" Alessio questions.

I sigh. "I can't explain it, but I don't know if I can go through with kidnapping her," I finally admit to not only my brothers but to myself. I have been in denial since the beginning.

There is silence on Alessio's end before he finally responds, "Fine, we will just have to find another way to get to Ronan."

I am relieved and thankful for my brothers for having my back on this. I don't know what pull Lily has on me but she's like a drug I can't get rid off.

Chapter 12

LILY

The next couple days have been amazing. I explained to Nico I am okay with him having a key to my place, but he needs to text me whenever he stops by.

He didn't question why I needed to know which I'm thankful for. I don't know what lie I would have had to come up with to explain it.

Every day since, Nico has come to my place in the evening, and we have dinner at my place and watch a show or movie.

We take turns picking the show. He groans every time I pick a reality show, but I can tell he is getting invested in the contestants. Not because he is cheering them on but he enjoys watching them embarrass themselves.

He has slept over every night as well. I put a pillow between us every night, but somehow I end up in Nico's arms in the morning. I have a feeling he is behind it, but he plays innocence each time I question him.

Truth is I like waking up in his arms. I feel safe whenever I am with him. He makes me happy and comforts me.

Every time I get worried about my wedding date nearing, I look at Nico and all the pain and worries disappear. Until he leaves and everything comes crashing back like a tsunami.

We've also crossed off a number of places I've wanted to visit the last couple of days. Today Nico plans on taking me to the Brooklyn Bridge.

I'm finishing get ready when I hear a knock on my door.

I know it's not Nico since he has a key. I quickly walk over to my door and with shaky hands I open the door.

My heart drops at seeing Ronan standing in the hallway. He pushes past me and walks into my apartment.

He looks around the apartment and, in a frenzy, I survey the room to make sure none of Nico's things are in plain view. He has a duffle bag full of his clothes in my room but that's about it.

Ronan turns towards me. "Have you been good, Lily?"

I nod quickly with my tongue feeling heavy. My heart feels like it's going to pop out of my chest.

Ronan looks at my outfit. I am wearing skinny denim jeans and a blue tank top. "Change into a nice dress. We are going to have dinner and I want you dressed more appropriately." I nod and quickly turn towards my room.

Once I enter my room, I close my door and kick Nico's duffle bag under my bed.

I grab my phone and quickly text Nico.

Something came up. Can't hang out tonight. Let's do something another day. Don't come to my apartment.

I grab a dark purple dress from my closet and switch my outfit in less then 30 seconds. I grab a pair of heels and walk out to the living room.

Ronan glances at me and nods in approval. "Let's go."

I quickly grab my purse from the counter and follow Ronan out.

The guard Carlo from the previous time is waiting in the hallway for us.

Ronan puts his arm around my waist and guides me into the elevator. His touch makes me want to flee out of my own body.

Once we get to the ground floor, Ronan guides me outside to the waiting SUV. I get in and Ronan follows suit.

I want to ask him where we are going but so far he is in a good mood and I don't want to piss him off by asking the wrong question.

A thought comes to my mind, he could be taking me back to that sleezy strip club. He had told that stripper he wanted me to suck him next time. I start to tremble at the thought of us going back there.

I look out the window to try and convince myself to think of something else. To my surprise we seem to be heading in the opposite direction.

Maybe we aren't going there. Maybe we are going somewhere worse.

Ronan is texting on his phone the entire time. I have the urge to ask where we are going but I bite the inside of my cheek to prevent myself from talking.

We leave the city and a few minutes later we pull up in front of a gate. The large steel gates open and we drive up a long driveway. At the end of the driveway is a large two-story mansion. It's as big as my family's in Chicago.

"Welcome to my home," Ronan says.

"This is your home?"

"Will be yours too in 2 and half months. Get used to it, since you will be spending most of your life in there." My *life*.

Ronan gets out of the SUV and the driver opens the door for me. I try and avoid making eye contact with the driver. Once I get out, Ronan comes around wraps his arm around my waist and heads towards the entrance of the house.

We walk into a large foyer that is all marble with two large stairs on each end of the foyer.

Ronan pulls me towards a hallway until we reach a large dining room.

There is large crystal chandelier hanging from the ceiling and underneath it is a table for about 20 people.

Ronan takes me to the end of the table and pulls out my chair as if he is some gentleman. I take a seat and Ronan takes the seat at the head of the table.

Ronan looks at his watch and drums his fingers on the table in waiting. I don't know who he is waiting for, but I pity the person knowing Ronan doesn't like to be kept waiting.

I look around thinking he is waiting for the servers. When I don't spot anyone, I'm about to offer I can go check on the food before he decides to beat the poor servers like he did me.

Just as I'm about to say something a small, dark blonde haired boy with blue eyes walks into the room. He looks to be around 12 or 13 years old.

"Your late," Ronan says with annoyance.

"I'm sorry, Uncle," says the young boy. He walks over to the chair across me and takes a seat.

"This is my nephew Killian." Ronan motions towards the boy. "Killian, this is going to be your aunt."

The little boy peers up at me from underneath his eyelashes and gives me a small smile.

I smile back at the boy. "It's nice to meet you, Killian."

"It would be nice if he was on time. Lily, what happens when I am kept waiting?" Ronan asks me.

I know the answer but don't want to say it. Killian takes a large gulp and looks down. He must know the answer as well.

"Lily?" Ronan warns.

The fear that crawls up my body at his tone scares me, but I can't get myself to say it. I know if I say it, it will condemn the young boy Killian to pain.

The servers enter with food but stop mid-way sensing the tension in the air. They hurriedly back out of the room.

Ronan shakes his head. "I will have to deal with you later, Lily." He turns to the young boy. "Killian, what happens if you keep me waiting?"

"Punishment," Killian says quietly with his head hung.

My heart breaks at seeing this young boy accept the punishment Ronan has decided he deserves.

"That's right." Ronan picks up the fork in front him which confuses me as there is no food on the table. Then Ronan stabs Killian in the back of his hand with the fork.

Killian screams in pain and I jump from my seat in shock causing my chair to go flying into the wall behind me. I grab a napkin from the table and run around the table towards Killian and place the napkin on the three puncture wounds on Kilian's hand from the fork.

I turn to face Ronan with disgust but get knocked back by a glass hitting the top of my head.

When I look up from the ground, I see Ronan standing above me. "Next time do as your told Lily, and I won't have to punish you." Ronan gets a call and he pulls out his phone. "I'll be back," he says before walking out of the dining room.

I feel something dripping from my head and hope it's just Ronan's drink from the glass. I touch the area and find my fingers red with blood.

"You're bleeding from your head," Killian sniffles while trying to hold in his tears.

"I'm fine. How is your hand?" I brush the shattered glass away from me and get on my knees to take a look at Killian's hand. Thankfully it's not bleeding a lot. The fork only made small puncture wounds. But I'm sure it still hurt a lot.

"It's fine and doesn't really hurt at all." Killian juts out his chin in bravery.

"You're Shay Fitzgerald's son, right?" I remember hearing about Ronan's brother, the former Irish mob boss getting arrested and sent to prison. After that Ronan took over.

Killian nods.

Ronan walks back into the dining room. "Time for dinner," he proclaims in excitement, as if he didn't just stab his young nephew and hit me over the head with a glass.

When he takes his seat he glances in my direction. "Get off the damn floor Lily, unless you plan on doing something more to my liking down there."

I push to my feet and walk back to my seat, trying to reel in my anger and disgust.

The servers come back in and place the food in front of us. Ronan feasts like the pig he is without a care. Killian nibbles on his food and I once again push my food around the plate due to my lack of appetite.

After 30 minutes Ronan gets another call and leaves the room again.

Carlo comes to the dining a few minutes later and tells me that Ronan asked for me to be taken back to my apartment.

I say goodbye to Killian before heading out. I worry for the little boy as he will be all alone in this house with that monster Ronan. But I know I can't help myself let alone him.

NICO

When Lily messaged me saying there are change of plans, I was furious. I knew what that meant. I confirmed with the soldier keeping an eye on Lily what I had assumed. Ronan was there.

It took all my reasoning to prevent me from acting out in anger. That and Carter physically blocking my way. I get up from my chair and start pacing the office.

"You shouldn't have gotten involved with her," Carter says.

I glare at him, "Don't you think I know that?"

"She was supposed to be a means to an end."

"I know that too," I say through clenched teeth. I can feel my muscles tightening with each second.

"Even if we don't use her to get to Ronan, she is still Ronan's fiancé. She will eventually marry Ronan. And not to mention you are married."

Carter is right. I made a mess of things and I don't know how to fix it. Even if I convince Lily to go against her parents and her family by not marrying Ronan, I can't offer her anything. I'm a married man and despite hating my bitch of a wife, we don't believe in divorce since we are Catholic. Lily would be condemning her family to war in return for nothing.

My phone rings and I look at the message. It's from the soldier keeping watch at Lily's apartment. She has returned.

"She's back alone at her place. I'm going over."

Carter shakes his head in disapproval but doesn't say anything to stop me. Probably for the best since I wouldn't listen to him anyways.

I drive over the speed limit and make it to Lily's apartment in less than ten minutes.

I head straight to her floor and use my key to walk into her apartment. She is not in the living room, so I walk into her room.

I see the bedroom bathroom light on and push open the door.

Chapter 13

LILY

Carlo dropped me off and I've changed into my sleepwear. However, the cut from the glass is still bleeding. I'm trying to figure out how to put a bandage in my hair since the cut is in my hairline on my left side, when the bathroom door swings open.

I'm startled at someone intruding into my bathroom and jump in shock but as soon as I see it's Nico, I sigh with relief.

Nico's eye bore into me and he looks at me with a pitied look. "What happened?"

"I fell again." Another lie I tell him. I've lost track of the number of lies I have told since the day I met him.

He doesn't say anything but just stares at me with that look that unsettles me. I don't need him to pity me. It's bad enough I pity myself.

I grab a bandage from the counter. "I just need a bandage and it should be fine."

Nico walks over to me and with the lightest touch tilts my head forward. "You need stitches."

I can't go to the doctor. It's hard enough to lie to Nico but lying to a doctor who sees injuries and cuts daily seems hard.

"I think it should be fine."

Nico picks me up and places me on the bathroom counter. "I know how to stitch up wounds. I can do it." He starts going through the first aid kit and pulls out a needle and sutures.

I'm not sure I should be letting him stitch me up. "I can go to the doctor tomorrow morning."

Nico looks up at me and gives a look that for the first time scares me to the core. I close my mouth shut.

He walks over to me and cleans around my wound with a cotton ball doused in disinfection and then tosses it to the side.

I feel the needle pierce the top of my head. It stings a lot. I grip onto Nico's suit jacket as he continues to stitch my wound. I feel a little tug and then Nico backs away. "Done."

I turn around and look in the mirror. I can't really see the sutures with my hair in the way but its seems to stop the bleeding.

I turn back towards Nico. "Thanks for stitching me up."

He doesn't say a word. He just cleans up the counter and places all the tools back into the first aid kit. I can't help but feel he is angry with me.

After cleaning up, he walks out of the bathroom without a word.

I slide off the bathroom counter and follow him out to the kitchen.

He takes out a beer from the fridge and walks into the living room and takes a seat on the couch. He takes a large swig from the beer and looks at the blank television screen.

I sway between my feet unsure what to do. "Is something wrong?" I finally ask.

Nico laughs. "Is something wrong? No Lily, nothing's wrong or maybe everything's wrong?"

I don't understand what he is saying. He isn't making much sense. But I can tell he is hurt and upset but I don't know about what and I don't like seeing him like this.

He has helped me by just being there for me and I hate that I can't help him.

I walk over to him and kneel in between his thighs. I place my hand on his knee and look up at Nico. "What's wrong?" I don't know if I can help but if I don't try, we won't know.

Nico looks down at me with such sadness. It tugs on my heart seeing him like this. He gently caresses my cheek with the back of his finger.

I grab hold of his hand as he pulls away. The warmth of his hand sending a spark down my spine.

I push up on to my knees and pull him towards me. I kiss him lightly on the lips, needing to feel him but also needing him to feel me. He kisses me back and pulls me up towards him on to his lap.

His hand grips my hair and he deepens the kiss.

My hands slide up his chest, and the heat from his body sends a tremor throughout my body. I know I should stop before it goes too far but I don't want to.

In that moment I decide I need this to be my choice. My decision. Not Ronan's to take once we are married.

I pull on Nico's shirt and he groans against my mouth. "Lily, we should stop."

I slide my hand down Nico's chest to his pants and start to unbuckle his belt. He grips my waist and picks me up. I wrap my legs around Nico's waist as he carries me towards my bedroom.

We fall onto my bed mattress hitting the soft sheets. Nico takes off his suit jacket and tosses it to the side. I pull at his shirt and unbutton it and that too goes flying to a corner in my room a few seconds later.

Nico grabs my silk camisole nightie and pulls it above my head. Next to go is my bra and underwear, until I'm completely naked.

I can feel the heat from Nico's intense stare. He kicks off his shoes and pulls down his dress pants and boxers in one swift motion. I can't help but gawk at his throbbing angry looking cock. The thought of something that large inside of me sends a shudder down my spine. Before I can even consider trying to figure out how it's even going to fit in me, Nico is on me again.

"Are you sure about this?" Nico asks.

"Yes," I breathe.

He parts my legs and guides his cock towards my opening. I halt at the sudden intrusion of a foreign object down there.

Nico kisses me again and then kisses the corner of my mouth before pushing in further. I grip his shoulder, digging my nails in from the pain.

He pushes in further slowly until he is fully in. I feel utterly stretched and full.

He slowly slides out and I flinch at the pain. He kisses my shoulder and pushes back in.

He slowly begins thrusting in and out mixing the pain with a slight pleasure.

After a few shallow thrusts, he begins to push in deeper and faster into me. I start to claw at his back from the sudden movement and pain.

Then all of a sudden, I feel a weird sensation like I am on a high and being pushed off a free falling cliff. I start to see stars as an intense pleasure washes over my body.

As I am coming down from the high, I feel Nico release inside me. After coming down from his own high, he collapses on top me as we both try to get our breathing under control.

After a few seconds, he pushes himself up and kisses me before rolling off me.

I feel a stinging pain when he pulls out of me. I push myself up to a sitting position and look between my legs.

There is pink dripping down my thigh and onto my sheets.

The realisation of what I did comes raining down on me hard and loud. I am no longer a virgin.

NICO

I roll off Lily and on to my back. She rises to a sitting position and looks down at her legs.

I follow her gaze and see she is staring at the blood mixed with the come in between her legs.

She pales. She gave her virginity to me. I know I should have stopped it but whenever she is around, I lose all my senses. But I have no regrets of taking Lily's virginity. She is mine.

Her eyes fill with tears and that angers me. She probably regrets giving it away to me. She must have wanted to save it for that fucker Ronan.

She sticks her hand out and touches her thighs lightly and a tear drops down her cheek. I get up in a sitting position in anger and grab hold of her hand. I want to shout at her she's mine so stop fucking crying.

She turns and looks up at with those enchanting eyes of hers filled with tears. I forget about my anger in that moment and I wrap an arm around her waist and pull her on to my lap. She wraps her arms around my neck and cries into the crook of my neck.

Her delicate body shakes against mine but being the selfish bastard that I am, I still have no regrets.

After crying herself out, Lily passes out in my arms in exhaustion.

I gently place her down on the bed and head over to the washroom and grab a wet washcloth.

I clean in between her legs and pull the blanket up to her shoulders. Once I discard the washcloth in the hamper, I return to bed and pull Lily to me. She is mine now and no one can take her from me.

Chapter 14

LILY

I wake up in Nico's arms. Last night after I decided to give something of mine that my papa has decided should be Ronan's, I regretted it.

Not that I gave it to Nico. I have no regrets about that. My body is mine to give and no one else's.

My regret has to do with what Ronan will do when he finds out I am no longer pure. He will probably kill me and I am okay with that. I made the decision to give my virginity away. But if he hurts Nico, I don't think I would be able to survive that. I have fallen for Nico and the thought of Ronan hurting him is unbearable.

I realized last night how selfish I have been. I didn't think about what Ronan would do to Nico once he finds out. This entire time I only thought of the punishment he would inflict on me. It didn't even cross my mind the danger I was putting Nico in.

I know I have to end this. For Nico's sake. He didn't sign up for this. He doesn't know about Ronan or what he is capable of.

He thinks I'm Lily Williams, a young normal single girl. Not a mafia princess engaged to a psychopath Irish mobster.

I try and pull myself away from Nico but his hold on me tightens.

"Stop moving," he says in a low sleep voice with his eyes still closed.

"I-I," I croak. My voice is shattering at the emotions filling me up at the thought of ending this.

Nico moans, "Don't tell me your still regretting last night."

Most people would be embarrassed after crying their eyes out after having sex for the first time. But embarrassment is very low on my list of concerns right now.

I push down the lump forming in my throat. "Nico, I don't think we should see each other anymore."

He opens his eyes and looks at me with a range of emotions going through his brown eyes. Then something shifts and something dark passes over his face. "That's not happening. You are mine now, Lily." His voice is even but strangely lethal.

I place my hands on his chest and try and push up, but he still doesn't loosen his arms. "Nico, you don't understand." I try and form an excuse or a lie he will believe.

I can't tell him the truth. Rule one of the mob is never tell an outsider anything about the mob. You never know who might go to the police. But mostly I don't want him confronting Ronan.

"I don't care. Try to run and I will chase you. Try to hide and I will find you. You are now mine."

A shiver goes down my spine from the piercing look in Nico's eyes that makes me think I'm in trouble.

He pulls me closer to him and kisses the top of my forehead. "Go to sleep."

Yeah, I am definitely in trouble.

After falling asleep, I wake up to an empty bed. Nico is gone. I get up and find a note on my bedside table.

Had to go to work. Will be back tonight.

Okay that gives me a couple hours to figure things out. First how the hell I can end this with Nico. Whatever the hell this is. I don't even know what our relationship status is. My boyfriend, my friend, or just some guy I had sex with.

Second, I need to grab the morning after pill from the pharmacy since I'm not on birth control.

I grab a shirt and sleep shorts and head towards the kitchen. I find another note on the counter.

Make sure you eat something proper and not just drink coffee.

I smile at the note. No one has cared to even ask if I ate or not back home.

The pain in my heart at losing Nico is unbearable. He was the only good thing in my life.

One way or another, I am going to lose him anyways. Either when Ronan finds out and kills him or when I have to end things to marry Ronan.

It's for the best if we end things now before we get any more invested. Not sure if that's possible considering I have completely and utterly fallen for Nico.

NICO

I got a text early this morning from Alessio advising me he has returned home with his family. I didn't want to leave Lily, but I needed to take care of things with Alessio.

I arrive at Alessio's penthouse. Mine and my brothers' penthouses are all in the same building. Alessio's penthouse is on the top floor, with mine and Gia's below his, and Carter's is below ours.

I take the exclusive elevator we all share to Alessio's and walk into his living room. I am greeted by my adorable niece Emma who comes running towards me.

"Uncle Nico!" she screams.

I pick her up into my arms and give her a kiss on the cheek. "Did you miss me?"

She nods her head. "Did you miss me?"

"Every day."

Alessio walks into the living room with his wife Anna behind him with baby Daniele in her arms. "Emma, why don't you help your mom out with Daniele?"

Emma wiggles in my grasp to be put down. I place her gently on the ground. "Okay." She turns and looks up at me. "We can play later."

I crouch down to her level. "Promise?"

"Promise." Emma smiles before running to Anna and grabs her free hand instantly.

I straighten as Anna smiles at me. "It's nice to see you again, Nico. Let's catch up later."

I give Anna a smile back. "Of course."

Alessio gives Anna a kiss before she takes Daniele, who is squirming in her arms, and Emma upstairs.

Before Alessio married Anna, he was different. At work he is still the same ruthless Capo but with her he is completely different.

It took him a long time to admit it but he loves and adores Anna. He is gentle and kind when she is around. Where with his first wife Maria, he was merely doing his obligations as husband.

Once Anna and the kids are upstairs, I face my brother. "Alessio, we need to talk."

"If it's about Lily Mancini, yeah we do."

"I will get you Ronan, I made you a promise and I will keep it. But I want to keep Lily out of this."

"I don't think that's possible. Word is spreading that you have someone on the side. It won't be long before someone puts a name to the face. Lily might not be well known in this city, but it only takes one person."

"I know. I just need time and your support with this."

Alessio doesn't say anything at first. "Okay."

"Okay?"

Alessio smiles. "Yeah, as long as we get Ronan, I don't care how. As for your relationship with Lily, I will support you. I don't remember the last time I've seen you this happy."

"Thanks, Alessio." Alessio has always put his family first and that includes me and Carter.

"You need to be more careful until we have things figured out. If anyone ever finds out you are seeing Lily, things could get bad. Not just for us but for Lily too. I doubt her family or Ronan would be okay with her associating herself with us. She is also the daughter of a Capo; they wouldn't take this well."

It doesn't matter. No one is taking Lily away from me.

Chapter 15

LILY

I'm heading to the grocery store and pharmacy when I run into Matt in the lobby of my apartment building.

He gives me a big smile. "Lily, how have you been?"

"Good," I lie.

"That's good." He hesitates before speaking, "I didn't know you had a boyfriend."

"Boyfriend?"

"That tall guy with brown hair and a suit that shows up here every evening and spends the night."

My cheeks go red at Matt noticing Nico has been spending the night here. "Can you do me a favor and not tell anyone you saw him?" I don't need word getting back to my parents or Ronan about this.

"Of course. I'm guessing your dad doesn't know, huh?"

My eyes widen. "My dad?" I didn't know Matt knew who my dad was.

"That older guy that shown up here a few times with a guard. He is your dad right?" Matt must think Ronan is my dad. I give him a nod. "What does he do for a living that he needs a guard?"

"Nothing important," I wave off the topic of Ronan's job description. "Can you do me another favor? Can you not tell my dad about my boyfriend?" Not sure which word feels weirder on my tongue. Calling Ronan my dad or Nico my boyfriend.

Matt nods. "Yeah no problem. If you like I can always give you a text message whenever your dad comes by, so you have a heads up in case your boyfriend is over."

I give Matt a wide smile. "That would be great!"

This way I don't have to worry about any surprise appearances from Ronan. Every time I hear a knock, I go into panic mode. I'm surprised I haven't lost all my hair from the stress. At least now I will have time to prepare if Matt texts me in advance.

Matt pulls out his phone. "What's your number?"

I quickly say my phone number to Matt who saves it on his phone and sends me a quick text so I have his number.

"Thanks Matt." I wave him goodbye as I head out to the store.

I'm back in my apartment with four huge bags full of groceries. It was a challenge carrying them back but Matt saw me struggling outside the building and helped me carry some of the bags back up to my apartment.

I pull out the groceries from the bags and place them on the counter. Nico had mentioned he loves lasagna and I decided to try and make it for him. Sort of like a last dinner before I break things off.

It hurts my heart ending things with Nico but it's for his safety. He has been so kind and caring towards me and I wanted to do something nice for him one last time.

It may not be anything big or extravagant but hopefully he still appreciates it.

I take out his favorite beer I've noticed him drinking a number of times and place it in the fridge. I then pull up instructions on my phone to cook lasagna. The family cook had taught me in the past, but it's been a few years since I've made it.

I learned to cook when I was younger since there was nothing else for me to do at home besides watch shows and movies.

My family was too busy for me and I never had any friends since they or their parents were afraid to be near me.

When I was in elementary school a rumor had spread that anyone standing next to me would get shot. After that everyone kept a distance from me.

I chop all the vegetables and meat and place them in a pan with the pasta. Once I'm done with the preparations, I turn on the oven and place the lasagna in there to bake.

I head to my bedroom and decide to get ready. I do my hair and makeup and change into a purple lilac dress. I'm finishing up fixing my hair when I hear the door open.

A few seconds later, Nico walks into my bathroom and wraps his arms around my waist from behind me. I lean my head back and I can't help but melt at seeing his handsome face.

He leans down and kisses the top of my head. "I smell something baking in the kitchen."

I turn in his grasp now facing him. "I wanted to do something nice for you because of last night."

I was an emotional crying mess and Nico still took care of me like he always does.

He leans down and gives me a kiss and I can't help but push myself up on my tiptoes and deepen it.

I hear the oven alarm go off, making me come to my senses. I pull away from Nico. "We should eat. The food will get cold."

He doesn't let go of me but instead looks into my eyes as if searching for something. "What are you up to?"

I go stiff in Nico's arms. "Nothing." It's like he can read my thoughts and feelings. I smile trying to reassure him. "Let's eat," I try again.

After a few seconds Nico lets me go but from the look on his face, I can tell he still suspicious.

We walk back into the kitchen, and I pull out the dishes and cutlery and place them on the small dining table. Nico places them out for me while I grab the lasagna and side salad I made. I place them in the middle of the table and go back to the kitchen and open the fridge. "Do you want a beer?" I turn around and ask Nico.

Nico takes a seat at the dining table and crosses his arms against his chest. He looks at me and assess me like I'm some puzzle he can't solve. It makes me feel uncomfortable, but I pull out the beer anyways and place it in front of him on the table.

I take a seat across from him and cut up a portion of lasagna and place one serving on Nico's plate and then one on mine.

Nico doesn't take his eyes off me. Instead, while keeping his entire focus on me, unscrews his beer and takes a drink. "Are you going to tell me what you're up to yet?"

I sigh. "Nothing, I just wanted to do something nice for you."

"Before?"

"Before what?"

"Drop the act, Lily. I can tell your up to something."

My eyes get watery at his harsh tone. I try and hold in the tears. I don't need a part two of me being an emotional mess after last night.

"Fuck," Nico swears before getting up from his chair and coming around the table. "I'm sorry I didn't mean to make you cry." He cups my cheeks with both his hands and leans down and kisses the top of my forehead.

I shake my head in his grasp. "No, you're right. I wanted to do something nice for you before I ended things."

His hands on my cheeks slightly tighten and a storm of emotions pass over Nico. He narrows his eyes at me. "Didn't I tell you that's not happening? You can't get rid of me. I'm not going anywhere."

I get up from my seat, not liking the height difference advantage Nico has. But even standing I only reach his chest.

"You don't understand," I cry. I don't know how to explain my situation. "There is someone else." Which is not a lie. There is someone else. Just not someone I want to be with, but I'm stuck with.

"And?" Nico says with a deadly calmness that surprises me. I didn't expect him to react like this. I assumed he would be mad or upset. Nico goes back to his chair and takes a seat. "Let's finish eating. I am not going anywhere, and you are no one else's but mine."

I'm still standing in a daze while Nico takes a bite of the lasagna. I've never broken up with anyone, but I don't think this is how it's supposed to go.

On shows or movies, when a person tries to end things, the other person barges out of the room in anger or sadness.

"Sit, Lily." Nico points towards my chair with his fork.

I slowly take my seat. Unsure of what I'm supposed to do now. We eat in silence while I try and make sense of what just happened. By the end of the meal, it still doesn't make sense.

Nico gets up and takes both of our dishes to the sink.

"So," I start, "I think you should go." I try again.

Nico whips his head back at me and then stalks towards me. His gaze holds something frightening. With each step he takes, my heart hammers in my chest.

But rather then run in fear, I stand still in anticipation. There is something about Nico, that scares me but also makes me want to get closer to him. Unlike with Ronan where I just want to run and never look back.

Once he reaches me, it feels like the air surrounding us is on fire. Nico slowly cups my cheek, and it feels like a scorching heat.

"You want me to go." He leans down barely touching my lips. "If I leave, I will not come back. Is that what you want?"

I hear him saying the words but I can't focus on what he is saying.

All I can think about is the heat that is going down my body. His lips continue to hover over mine in a tease.

I can't take it anymore and push up and finally lock our lips together. Nico's hand is in my hair, and he tilts my head to get better access to my lips.

I wrap my arms around Nico's neck and push my body against his. I feel his erection rub against my stomach and I lose all senses.

Nico spins me around and pushes me face down on the dining room table. I'm trying to catch my breath when I hear him unzip. He pulls my dress up to my waist and pushes my lace panties to the side. His finger rubs up against my sensitive folds and I quiver at his touch.

I feel his tip near my entrance, but he doesn't push in. Instead, he rubs his tip up and down and I shake at the sensation. I get the urge to push back.

Nico leans forward to my ear. "Still want me to leave?"

I know I should scream yes leave but I can't while he is playing with me. He nudges his tip slightly into my opening and I'm ready to break.

"I need an answer, Lily," Nico says.

I'm about to come apart at the seams when he pulls back slightly.

Screw this. I dig my nails into the table and push back, filling myself up.

I hear Nico chuckle behind me. He begins to pull in and out in hard shallow thrusts. With each thrust I am being pushed further up against the table when Nico wraps his arm around my waist to keep me in place.

I can feel an orgasm building and I push myself up from the table sending Nico deeper into me at the new angle.

I feel Nico tense up and then pulsate before releasing inside me. I too follow soon after in my own bliss and collapse onto the table as I come down from my orgasm. Nico kisses my shoulder blade. "I gave you an out, Lily. This was your one and only. Now you are mine. Accept it."

My face is pressed against Nico's chest and my naked body against Nico's. This is definitely not how you end things.

I trace my fingers on the scars and cuts on Nico's chest. He has a number of them scattered around his body.

I had noticed them before but didn't have the courage to ask.

I look up at Nico. "How did you get these scars?"

Nico takes a heavy swallow. "A car accident."

I trace the long scar on his upper bicep; it looks like the one my brother got when he was stabbed a few years back.

My papa had sent him on his first job and he made the mistake of looking away from the man he was supposed to kill, giving him the chance to stab him. I remember crying near his bed at the thought of the only person who remotely cared about me dying. Thankfully I was just being dramatic and it wasn't that bad.

Now I have a second person whom I love and care for.

I can try ending things again, but I have a feeling we will just end up in the same spot. He said he wasn't going to let me go. I believe him.

At least I have some time. My wedding with Ronan isn't for another two months.

Maybe Nico will get bored with me and break up with me on his own. For some reason that sends a pain through my heart.

Two months. I have two months to get Nico to break up with me and lose the one good thing I have.

Chapter 16

NICO

It's been a couple weeks since Lily tried to end things. I gave her a choice to end it. Even if she did go through with it, I don't think I would have been able to let her go. Regardless she doesn't get a say anymore.

Since that night, things have been back to normal. Or as normal as it can possibly get.

After I finish work, we spend our evenings back at her apartment having dinner and watching something on the television. We never finish whatever we are watching since we end up in bed before it is done.

Ronan hasn't shown up in Lily's place in a while which makes it easier for me not to go into a raging episode.

The thought of him touching Lily or hurting her makes me want to go on a murderous killing spree.

Instead, I have been taking out my anger for all the times Ronan has laid a hand on Lily on his men. We have killed over a dozen Irishmen the last few weeks and burned down one of his businesses. Our retaliation is probably what has kept him busy and away from Lily.

According to one of our lookouts, he hasn't left his house in weeks. The one and only time he did leave was to visit his brother Shay in prison.

He took a dozen guards with him and only took main roads, preventing us from attacking him in route.

Lily and I are on the couch watching a UFC fight. She has her head on my lap and is completely dazed out. I know she still wants to end things because of her upcoming marriage to Ronan but I don't give her the chance.

I play with her silky chocolate brown hair when she turns to face me. "I want to go out," she pouts.

Since I found out rumors are spreading of me seeing Lily, I have been keeping a low profile. No one knows who Lily is here in New York but I can't risk it.

Not to mention if someone recognizes me and tells Lily, I don't know what I would do. My brothers and I have been trying to find a solution where I can be with Lily but so far, we have come up empty handed.

"It's getting late. We can go out another day," I try and persuade her.

She pushes to her feet and walks into her bedroom in anger. I should go after her but I'm too busy looking at her ass in those tight denim shorts she wears.

A few seconds later she comes out wearing sneakers.

"Where are you going?" I ask.

"If you don't want to go out, I'll go by myself." Lily grabs the keys off the counter and makes her way towards the door.

I chase after her and grab her wrist. "We can go out tomorrow."

"No, I'm tired of this apartment. I want to go out and see things. Who knows when I'll be able to go out again." Her eyes widen slightly. "I mean, you can't take things for granted."

She tries to pull away free from me, but I don't let her go. "I'll take you out tomorrow to a restaurant for dinner and we can even go to Central Park again." I'm going to have to plan this properly in order to make sure we don't get seen, but for Lily, I will do anything.

"Fine," she finally caves. I pull her back to the couch and we settle back in.

LILY

Nico is taking me out to eat today. I'm a bit excited since I haven't been out in a while. Nico and I have been spending all of our time at my place and at first I didn't mind. I could be living in a cave with Nico and I would be happy.

As we were watching a UFC fight last night, the date on the top of the screen reminded me I'm running out of time.

In about 2 weeks, I'm supposed to marry Ronan. I still haven't ended things with Nico, not that he would let me.

Every time I even remotely bring up ending things, he finds a way to stop it somehow.

I had hoped he would grow bored of me, but that doesn't seem to be the case.

I felt like my walls were caving in and I needed to get out of my place. It was dumb of me to try and go out so late. I just wanted to go out and blend into the rest of world and feel normal for once, even if it's for a short time.

Nico had texted me earlier stating he was going to take me to a nice restaurant tonight.

I did my hair in soft waves and decided on a red strappy dress with a backless back.

I had bought the dress last year in hopes of being able to wear it out one day but like the rest of my clothes it's been sitting in my closet.

Besides going to school and the occasional party I went to with my family, I never had a reason before now to dress up.

I walk back into the living room to grab my purse and phone when I hear the door open. Nico walks in and looks striking as always.

He walks over to me and gives me a kiss. "Ready to go?"

I nod. "I just need to grab my purse and phone." I turn around to grab my things from my counter when I hear an inaudible sound come from Nico's throat. I turn and face Nico and see his eyes are dark.

"I'm ready to go," I say once I have my things in my hand.

"Don't you want to grab a jacket?"

"It's August, not to mention hot outside."

I would die of a heatstroke if I wore a jacket in this weather. I've had the air conditioner blasting on full since yesterday and for some reason I can't stop feeling hot.

Nico crosses his arms. "Either wear a jacket or change into something else."

"You can't be serious."

He is. Nico doesn't budge and I don't have it in me to fight him. The heat has made me sluggish and exhausted. I grab a jacket from the closet and put it on. "There. Happy?"

Nico smiles, pleased. "Very."

We head downstairs and pass by Matt. I know Nico doesn't like him for some reason. Being annoyed at Nico for making me wear a jacket I decide to wave at Matt as we leave.

Nico growls next to me and wraps his arm around my waist as we walk out. Once in the car, I turn on the air conditioner on full blast. I can feel the balls of sweat forming on my forehead. At this rate I really am going to have a heat stroke.

I start fanning myself with my hand, but I can't seem to cool down. Nico turns to me with a worried expression. "Lily, are you okay?"

"I'm fine. Just a bit hot."

"Do you want me to open up the windows?"

"No, I should be okay with the air conditioning."

We pull up in front of a restaurant after a short drive. I quickly open the door to try and get some air in. I take a step out of the car and feel lightheaded and tumble forward. Nico is beside with one arm wrapped around my waist and the other holding my arm.

"You clearly are not okay. Get back in the car." Nico nudges me back into the car seat and I feel myself collapse into the leather seat of his car. I don't have the energy to move or walk. Nico gets in and starts the car up again.

"I'm fine, let's go back to the restaurant."

Nico frowns in my direction. "You are not fine. We are going to the hospital."

Nico is being ridiculous. I'm about to open my mouth and argue against going to the hospital when Nico turns to me and gives me a look that makes me glue my mouth shut.

Sometimes he can be the sweetest and most charming guy I know and then all of sudden with one look he makes me fear him. You would think there's two different Nico's.

We arrive in front of the hospital and Nico gets out first and comes around to help me out. I want to tell him I can walk on my own but my legs feel like they're made out of jelly.

Once we walk into the emergency room a nurse asks for my insurance information and ID. I give my fake ID, but Papa didn't provide me with fake insurance papers. Even if he did, it is probably best I don't use it since he would be notified I am in the hospital.

I also can't use my credit card since that would also be reported to Papa. He would have a billion questions about this.

I'm about to tell the nurse I'm fine and don't need to be checked out when Nico hands the nurse his credit card. I want to stop him, but he still has that look that makes me keep my mouth shut.

After a few minutes the nurse takes me to a waiting bed in the emergency room.

"The doctor will be here shortly. If you need anything there is a button to your left you can press to call one of the nurses," the kind nurse informs me before closing the curtain and going back to work.

Noticing Nico doesn't have that look anymore I finally get the courage to speak. "I don't need to be here. I just felt hot because of the stupid jacket you made me wear."

"I made you wear a jacket because your back was on full display for all men to see. Besides it's not even hot today. The weather has shifted to fall."

Right, fall is just around the corner, along with my wedding date.

The curtain is pushed aside and a doctor comes in. "Miss Williams, I am doctor Lee. I heard you almost fainted."

"It's nothing. I was just feeling hot and tumbled." I glare up at Nico. This is all his fault. I didn't need to wear this jacket or had to come here.

"Well let's still have a look at you." The doctor listens to my heart. Checks my breathing and then takes a blood sample. All the while Nico stands in the corner watching the doctor like a hawk.

"I will be back once I have the results. It should take no more than an hour." Dr. Lee walks out and closes the curtain behind him.

Great, now I am stuck here for an hour. We could be out having dinner or doing anything but sitting here.

"If you're hungry, I can grab you something from the cafeteria?" Nico suggests.

"No, I don't want to eat cafeteria food. I want to go out and eat at a nice restaurant like normal people."

Nico walks over to my hospital bed and leans down and kisses the top of my head. "We can go out once the doctor informs us you are okay."

I cross my arms over my chest and give him a deadly look. Or what I think is a deadly look but probably more of a look a petulant child would give.

Nico just smiles at my failed look and gives me another kiss on the top of my head. Damn him.

After waiting 45 minutes, the doctor returns.

"Miss Williams, so it looks like you are healthy and fine," says

Dr. Lee.

I smirk up at Nico for overreacting.

"What caused her to faint then?" Nico questions.

Dr. Lee looks at Nico and then at me. "Miss Williams, maybe we should have this conversation alone."

Nico narrows his eyes at the doctor. "Why, what's wrong?"

"It's fine. Say whatever you would like to tell me," I tell the doctor.

Dr. Lee clears his throat. "According to the blood test, you're pregnant. It's still early in the pregnancy but you're about one month pregnant."

The doctor starts talking about how pregnant woman tend to feel hot during their pregnancy due to a higher heartrate that increases blood pressure, but I can't focus. All I can think about is I'm pregnant.

I've been taking morning after pills I got from the drug store a few blocks down from my place but I must have taken them incorrectly or missed one.

The doctor stops talking and looks at me. He must see the panic on my face.

"Miss Williams, there are also other options. It is still early in the pregnancy," Dr. Lee begins.

"Other options?" Nico interrupts. Nico glares down the doctor in anger. "I think that's enough. We don't need any other options."

"Well, if there is nothing else, Miss Williams, you are free to leave. I recommend making an appointment with an obstetrician once you get home." Dr. Lee hands out my discharge paperwork and Nico grabs it from Dr. Lee with more force then necessary.

After Nico finishes my paperwork, he helps me out of the hospital bed and towards his car.

We don't say a single word to each other the entire ride back to my apartment. Once we get back to my apartment, I walk straight to my bedroom and remove my clothes.

I don't bother to pick them up or place them in the hamper. I leave them lying on the ground and change into my sleepwear.

Once I am changed, I crawl into bed and lay down. I don't sleep or move. Just stare at the ceiling. My mind seems to have gone blank.

Nico comes over to my bed and hovers over me. I don't know what to say to him. I don't even know what to say to myself.

He leans down and kisses my forehead like he always does. "It's going to be okay. I'll figure this out." I look into his brown eyes, and I know he means it. But he doesn't realize the mess we truly are in because of me.

He straightens and turns off the light. "I'll be back. You just rest." He leaves, closing the door behind him.

Chapter 16

NICO

I get back in my car and just sit there and grip my steering wheel tightly. If I could rip it off the dashboard of my car, I would.

When the doctor said Lily was pregnant, I was excited at first. I was going to be a father. My precious Lily was carrying our child.

Then the doctor began talking about other options, as if having an abortion is even an option. Then I saw the look in Lily's eyes and I knew she didn't have the same excitement I did.

She was scared and in pain. She is supposed to marry Ronan in less than two weeks, and she was pregnant with my child.

Me and my brothers have been trying to get Ronan for weeks now but have failed each and every time.

Ronan wasn't getting his hands on Lily regardless but now that she is pregnant, I won't let him even get near her.

I start my car and start driving towards Encore. I need to speak to Alessio and Carter. They need to know.

I pull up in front of Encore. It's Friday night and there is a long line around the block of people trying to get in.

I get out of my car and make my way towards the entrance. The bouncer at the front nods at me and I give a curt nod back before making my way past them.

The music is loud as it bounces against the large club walls. It is filled with people dancing to the music or getting drunk at the bar.

As I make my way through the club, I notice women eyeing me and trying to get my attention.

In the past I would have given them 5 minutes but now I get the urge to shove them away.

I look up at the second floor that looks like an entire black wall but is actually a window from Alessio's office. He is probably up there looking down at me now.

I climb up the stairs and make my way to Alessio's office and hesitate at his door.

I know my brother will have my back no matter what, but I also know I really fucked things up.

I finally push open the door to finally face him.

Alessio is sitting at his desk with Carter on the leather couch on the other end of the room.

Alessio looks up at me. "I saw you come up. I'm surprised to see you here considering the last several weeks you've been spending your nights with Lily."

I open my mouth to speak but a large lump in throat stops me.

Carter stands up from the couch. "What's wrong?"

I push the lump down and force myself to talk. "Lily's pregnant."

Alessio stands and comes around his desk. "Are you sure?"

I nod, not able to force anymore words out.

"Fuck," Carter swears. "This is bad."

I don't need to be reminded. I look up at my older brother Alessio. "I need your help. I don't know what to do."

Alessio walks over to me and places a hand on my shoulder.

"Don't worry, we will figure this out."

LILY

I barely slept last night. I woke up in a terror after having a nightmare of Ronan killing Nico for my betrayal.

Nico sent me a text message stating he is at work, but he will be dropping by this evening to check up on me.

I'm making myself some tea, trying to figure out a way to get out of this mess I created.

I decide it's time I fess up. Nico needs to know the danger he is in. I considered running away but Papa or Ronan would eventually find us. There is no running from the mob. Besides I'm sure Nico doesn't want to leave his family or life here.

I realise I don't even know anything about Nico's family. In fact, I know very little about him. I hadn't asked about his family or life, fearing he might ask me questions.

At that time, I didn't want to lie to him with some made up stories but now I regret not asking.

Does he have any brothers or sisters? Do his parents live in the city or another state? What are they like?

My stomach growls loudly in the silent apartment. Since we skipped dinner last night, I'm starving. I don't have it in me to make anything.

I place my mug of tea in the sink and grab my purse and keys and decide to grab food from the bistro down the street.

I get to the bistro and order hordes of food. I think I'm secretly trying to eat my stress away but I don't care at this point.

After filling myself up on food I walk back to my apartment. My steps feel heavier the closer I get.

As if staying away from the apartment could solve all my problems. I need to face my problems and come up with a solution. If there is even a solution.

I walk into the lobby of apartment and see a curly haired brunette with a lot of makeup shouting at Matt.

Matt points in my direction and the brunette whips her head at me. She zeros in on me and charges at me like a bull running at their target. I'm about to ask who she is when all of a sudden, she raises her hand and slaps me across the cheek.

"You homewrecking whore! You think you can sleep with my husband and I wouldn't find out about it," she shouts.

I'm confused about what she is talking about and thrown off by her attack. "I think you have the wrong person."

"Don't lie to me! I know you're sleeping with my husband," she scoffs.

Her face is full of rage, but I don't understand why. I'm the one who got hit for no reason.

"You got the wrong person and I don't know your husband," I try and reason with her. I don't need this right now, I have my own problems to deal with.

"You don't know Nico Vitale? Liar, I knew you were lying. Your face says it all. Stop seeing my husband or the next time it won't just be a slap," she warns before shoving me with her shoulder and walking away.

I am left stunned in the middle of the lobby. Nico is married and his last name is Vitale. The only Vitale I know of is the Vitale family who is at war with the Irish.

Matt comes running towards me. "Are you okay? I didn't know she was going to slap you. If I did, I would have never told her who you were."

I don't respond and just walk past Matt and head towards the elevator. I feel like I am in a daze.

Nico can't be married or be a Vitale. All of a sudden, the pieces start fitting together.

KIARA MORGAN

My mama was right. I am stupid and naïve.

Chapter 17

NICO

I am at Encore with Alessio and Carter trying to figure out a way out of this mess I created. I can't let Lily go and now that she is pregnant, I have to move quickly. Her wedding date is less than two weeks away.

"There is no way we can get to Ronan right now and we can't offer anything to Lorenzo Mancini that would make him break his alliance with the Irish," Alessio points out.

Alessio is right. Lorenzo arranged a marriage with his daughter with a boss of the Irish mafia for a reason. In our world, marriage is a way for both parties to gain power.

We could offer Lorenzo a better deal but he wouldn't take it as there is no guarantee we would keep our end unless we formed an agreement through marriage. That would mean Lily would have to marry someone within the organization.

Since Alessio is married and I'm stuck to that bitch Gia, the only option would be Carter to marry Lily. Which I hate the thought of.

But even then, Lorenzo might refuse since Carter is only an enforcer within the organization while Ronan is boss of the Irish mafia.

We're trying to come up with a way to deal with Ronan when the office door flies open.

Gia walks in with her smug face. Or maybe that's just her face. She has gotten so much work done lately, I'm surprised her face hasn't fallen off. She looks like her face is being pressed against a window with all the Botox she had injected in.

I don't have time for her games. "What the fuck are you doing here?"

Gia crosses her arms and walks towards me. "Is that any way to talk to your wife?"

I roll my eyes. "Leave or I will have one of the guards drag you out." I have more important shit to deal with then her right now.

"I just came by to tell you, I dealt with your whore so don't bother seeing her again." Gia smirks.

"What are you talking about?" She can't be talking about Lily. There is no way she could have found out about her.

Gia just stands there were that annoying smile of her playing coy.

Alessio rises from his chair. "Gia, stop with the fucking games and tell us what you did."

"My papa told me you were seeing some whore behind my back, so I had my brother follow you one night as you visited that little whore you have hidden away." Fuck, fuck, fuck!

I grab hold of Gia's upper arms. "What the fuck did you do?" I'm barely holding my anger in from ripping Gia's head off.

"Let go of me, you're hurting me." Gia tries to wiggle out of my hold. But I don't let go.

"What the fuck did you do!" I shout in her face.

She startles at my reaction but quickly rages. "I went to your whore and told her to stay the fuck away from my husband and made sure she got the message with a nice slap." Gia looks so proud of herself, but I want to strangle her right here.

I push her away to the side and she topples in her heels falling to the ground while I quickly run out of the club. I need to get to Lily. I hear Alessio calling my name behind me, but I don't have time.

I get to Lily's apartment and walk in. She is sitting on the couch motionless.

"Lily," I try.

"Don't," she croaks. "You're married."

"I can explain."

She looks up at me with red, tear filled eyes. "What's your last name?"

Fuck. I don't respond. Her eyes are full of so much pain. Pain I wish I could take away, but I know I'm to blame for this.

Lily continues, "It's Vitale, right?"

I nod in confirmation since I can't seem to open my mouth. Anything I say I fear might make things worse.

"Did you know who I was from the beginning?"

I walk over to her and crouch in front of her. "Lily," I grab her hand, but she quickly pulls away from me.

Lily gets up and steps away from me. "Did you?" Her voice is cracking as tears fall down Lily's beautiful face.

"I did." I finally tell her the truth.

Lily's eyes flash with a mixture of pain, sadness and hurt. Then right in front of my eyes, I watch the woman I have fallen in love with break into pieces. Lily falls to her knees and covers her face with her hands as she lets out an agony filled cry. Her body trembles as she slowly falls apart in the middle of her living room.

I feel like my heart is being ripped into pieces at seeing her like this. The ache in my chest is the most painful thing I have ever felt. I have been tortured and stabbed by our enemies, but right now I would rather get stabbed a thousand times than see Lily like this.

I kneel down in front of her and lightly touch her hand but she flinches away from me. Her reaction to my touch pierces through me.

"Don't," she seethes. "Leave. I want you to leave!" Her voice rising with each word.

"I can't."

She rises to her feet and points a shaky finger in my direction. "You approached me to get to Ronan, didn't you? Your family is at war with the Irish. I was just a means to an end. Admit it." More tears fall down her cheek.

I straighten to my full height. "Yes."

Her brows furrow. "Why?" Her beautiful face filled with such confusion and pain.

"We needed to get to Ronan. We thought we could use you to get to him. But as I got closer to you, I grew feelings for you. My brothers and I changed the plan and will get Ronan another away without involving you."

I try and take a step towards Lily but she takes one back away from my reach.

"Leave." Her voice is emotionless, and her emerald eyes are empty. She was pure and innocent, and I ruined her.

"I'll leave but I'm going to come back. When I said you are mine, I meant it. You can't run or hide from me."

She doesn't look at me. Instead, she stares at the wall behind me. I will give her time and space for now.

I caused her this pain, but I will come back for her.

LILY

I sit in darkness for hours on the couch. This entire time I was worried about Nico getting hurt but in reality, he is as just as dangerous as Ronan if not more.

He destroyed me, and I hate him for that.

The Vitale family is ruthless. I heard their Capo butchered the entire Yakuza from the east coast a few years back. Something that is not done easily by anyone.

VENGEFUL PRINCE

I have always tried to keep away from the mafia side of my family's life since I blamed them for having no friends or life. Now I wish I had taken more of an interest. If I had, maybe I could have realized sooner who Nico really was.

Everything is making more sense now. The scars on his body, his car, his job, even his presence alone. I could feel something deadly and dangerous about Nico, but I let myself get consumed with his charming and kind side.

For all I know that was all an act to fool me. And he did. I let myself fall for a man who wants to kill my future husband.

I was nothing to him. Yet I gave him everything.

After a couple hours of sitting in the dark, I finally come up with a plan. It's a stupid plan but it's all I have.

I call my papa from my phone. He picks up after several rings.

"Lily, is everything okay?" His voice is filled with concern, but I know it's not for me. He is worried about this alliance.

"Papa, I think I need to be moved."

"Why, what's wrong?"

"I saw someone odd outside my apartment today. He looked Italian."

I didn't see anyone but if Nico knew from the start who I was, it means my location has been compromised. I'm sure they have someone watching my place even now especially if they are after Ronan.

"Are you sure?"

"I am, Papa. I was going to leave but I don't want him following me if he is working for the Italians."

"Lock your door and stay there. I'm going to call Ronan and have him move you." The call disconnects a second later.

A few minutes later, I get a call from Ronan. I pick it up hesitantly. "Hello?"

"Lily, it's me." Ronan. "I have a team of guards coming to pick you up. I am going to move you to a safe house until the wedding."

"Okay. Thank you." I don't want to thank him. I hate him but for once I need to be smart.

Once we hang up, I pack a small bag of clothes for me to take. I hear a knock on the door and go to answer it. It's Ronan's guard Carlo.

"Boss asked me to take you to a safe house."

"Okay, give me a second." I go back into the living room and look around for anything I might need. There is nothing. I toss my phone on the counter and walk out.

Chapter 18

NICO

I'm at Carter's penthouse waiting for Lily to forgive me. I don't know how much time she needs but I do know she needs time.

Watching her in so much pain was the most excruciating thing I've ever experienced in my life.

I wanted to make it all better and tell her I would fix it, but I couldn't get the words out. I don't know I can fix this.

Carter walks into the living room with two beers in his hand and passes one to me. I grab it instantly and take a large swig.

I knew one day Lily would have to find out, but I wanted to tell her, to make her understand.

"She will forgive you," Carter says before taking a seat across from me on the couch.

Carter's phone rings and he pulls it from his pocket. His eyebrows furrow before answering. He doesn't say anything but just listens to whatever the person on the other end is saying.

Carter rises to his feet. "Did you follow them?... What do you mean you lost them?" Carter hangs up the phone and then looks at me. "There's a problem. Ronan's guards came to pick up Lily and we lost track of her."

"What?" I push to my feet, "What do you mean you lost track of her? Find her!" I shout.

"I have soldiers looking for her now but…."

I don't let Carter finish his sentence. I grab my keys and head to the elevator. I need to find Lily.

Carter follows after me. "Wait for me, I'm coming with you. If Ronan is there or his men, you're going to need back up."

He's right. But no one is getting in my way from getting to Lily.

We get to her apartment and Carter and I take out our guns before entering. Once we enter, we slowly make our way through each room. It's empty. She's not here.

I send her a text asking her where she is right now and I hear a ping from the kitchen. I turn and find her phone laying on the kitchen countertop.

Fuck. If she left her phone here, we can't even trace it to find her location. She is really gone.

Carter places a hand on my shoulder. "Don't worry. We will find her."

Chapter 19

LILY

We pull up to a small brownstone house in Brooklyn. Carlo opens the door for me, and I step out to get a better view. The house is beautiful and quaint. I could imagine families living here.

My heart pinches at the thought of families.

I am pregnant with the enemy's baby about to marry a monster.

I take a deep breath and walk up the short steps to the front door.

The door flies open to a man I have not seen before. "The boss has been waiting for you." The man has a bit of an Irish accent.

I nod and follow the man into the house. We walk past some stairs and arrive in the living room.

Ronan is sitting across another man with peppered hair.

Once I enter, Ronan looks up, "Lily, I'm glad you made it here safe." He rises to his feet and comes towards me. I flinch and back away from him, but he wraps his arms around me. "Come sit. I'm sure it must have had a scary experience finding out the Italians found you." He guides me to the couch, and I take a seat unsure what to do.

Ronan takes a seat next to me and places a hand on my thigh. I get the urge to push him away but hold it in.

"I want you to meet Patrick, my second in command." Ronan motions to the man sitting across from us. "We were just discussing how to kill those Italian fuckers."

My heart hurts at the thought of Nico getting hurt. I hate what he did but despite it all I would never wish death on him. My stupid heart won't let me.

I clear my throat. "That is what I wanted to talk to you about." I peer up at Ronan and try to gauge his reaction for me speaking. So far, he hasn't beat me up so I continue, "I know our wedding is in two weeks, but I worry they might plan something. Maybe we should push up the wedding date."

Ronan raises an eyebrow and smirks at my suggestion. "And here I thought you didn't want to marry me." Ronan drums his fingers against the armrest. "What do you think, Patrick?"

Patrick takes a sip of his drink before responding, "It might be a good idea to get married sooner. Our alliance with the Mancini with finally be in place and we would throw the Vitales off guard. Not to mention Lily won't have to stay in hiding here anymore. You can move her to your place without her father being worried about her being tainted."

Little do they know I am already tainted.

Ronan rubs his chin in thought. "I'll speak to Lorenzo tonight." He turns to me, "In the meantime, you can go upstairs and rest."

I nod and push to my feet and head out of the living room.

Once I have left the living room, I hear Patrick and Ronan speaking in hushed voices. I can't help myself but stop and listen to their conversation.

"You have quite a mess here, Ronan," Patrick says. "Shay hasn't been pleased of hearing about the ongoing conflict with the Vitales for a while now."

I hear a glass slam on the table causing me to jump. "I am the leader now, not my brother. Why are you even discussing this with him? Have you been seeing my brother behind my back?"

There is silence for a few seconds before Patrick speaks, "You may be the leader right now but that is only until Shay returns. Don't forget that, Ronan. I have known Shay for over 30 years and I consider him my best friend and brother. I have gone to see Shay and that is only because you have failed to keep him updated on Killian."

"I have been raising Killian as I would my own son." Ronan's voice is filled with barely contained anger. If the way Ronan has treated Killian is how he would raise his own children, it sends a chill down my body. I place my hand on my stomach at the thought of what he would do to my baby.

"And that is what I am worried about. I know how you are. He is still a child and not ready for your *teachings*."

Ronan laughs. "You are telling me how I should raise a child when you haven't even seen yours in over 15 years. If it will get you to shut up, I will provide Shay with updates on Killian more often."

I consider standing and listening some more to their conversations but the heavy feeling in my gut nudges me to walk away.

I make my way up the stairs and find a room to occupy.

Once I am settled, I get into bed and try to sleep but my mind is filled with hundreds of thoughts and my heart crumbles with each passing thought.

Chapter 20

LILY

Ronan and my father agreed with me about pushing up the wedding date. My wedding date was then changed from 2 weeks to less then 3 days.

In those 3 days everything had to be rearranged. From the church to the reception venue.

Most people were accommodating to the sudden change in date but I think it had more to do with their fear of my groom and the amount of money being thrown at them to pull it off.

Today is my wedding day.

I had loathed the idea of my wedding from the moment I found out and here I am, praying for this day to come sooner.

My dress is modest and simple with long lace sleeves and a sweetheart neckline.

I had envisioned my wedding dress since I was a child. Back then I dreamt of getting married to man who loved and cherished me for once.

As I look at the mirror, I see and feel nothing. I am nothing more than a shell trying to survive.

My mama comes into the bridal suite and looks at me with awe. This is the first time she has ever looked at me like this.

For years I have begged and pleaded for her and papa's attention and for once I have it but can't accept it.

I betrayed them and they don't even know it.

"You look beautiful, Lily. Of course, you would be on the happiest day of your life. My wedding day was mine, that and when I had your brother."

Of course, she wouldn't mention when she had me. I don't say anything or react, instead I turn and face the mirror.

I wouldn't be surprised if a part of her knew I wasn't worthy of her love and attention. The first chance I was away from home I risked everything.

My mother continues talking about something, but I don't hear it. All I hear is how unworthy I am. I am a traitor and a failure to my family.

"Lily, are you listening to me?" I hear my mama ask. I turn to face her, and she continues with whatever she is going on about without waiting for a reply from me.

I hear a knock on the door before it opens and my brother Enzo pops his head in. "Is it okay if I come in?"

I give him a small nod giving him permission to enter.

My brother turns to my mama. "Papa is looking for you."

My mama turns and heads to the door. "I'll be right back." I want to tell her don't bother, I don't deserve it, but I keep it to myself with all the other secrets and betrayals.

My brother stands to the side of the room staring at me. "You remember what I told you, Lily. Two or three years only. I promise." His emerald eyes, similar to mine, scan over my face. I wonder if he can see the shame on it.

I raise my head to my brother and instantly my eyes well up with tears. I try and force them away. "Enzo, I don't think I will make it that long. Instead make me another promise."

Enzo's body goes rigid before responding, "Anything."

I smile at how quickly he agreed. My older brother who I wish I could have spent more time with.

"If I have any children in the future, promise me if something happens to me you will protect them and take care of them. Do not leave them with Ronan."

Enzo stares at me for a beat before answering, "I promise."

With that I know at least my child will be safe. Seeing how Ronan is with Killian, I fear for my child's safety.

Another knock on the door is heard and my brother goes to open the door. He turns back to me. "Lily, they're almost ready for you."

I swallow down the pain and hurt. "Okay, just give me some time alone and then I will be ready."

NICO

Today is Ronan and Lily's wedding date. We just found out an hour ago that they had pushed up the wedding to today.

I am pacing in Alessio's home office like an animal locked in a cage.

"Nico, why don't you take a seat?" Alessio says.

"Take a seat! Lily is about to marry Ronan as we speak!" I shout. I know it's not my brother's fault, it's mine. I should have moved Lily to a safe spot weeks ago, away from Ronan.

"Nico," Carter tries, "I know how you feel." He does. He lost the woman he loves but the thought of me losing Lily is tearing me apart from the inside.

"We need to attack the church," I say.

Alessio and Carter don't say anything.

"If we go now, we can still make it."

Alessio finally speaks up, "We can't attack the church. There would be to many civilians in there and not to mention Ronan has his entire security detail watching. It would be a bloody mess if we attacked."

I know he is right. But all I can think about is not losing Lily.

"Maybe we don't attack," Carter begins. "We might be able to get one or two of us into the church without anyone noticing. If you can convince Lily to leave with us we might be able to get out unscathed and without detection."

I take in what Carter is saying. It's a risky move but it's all we have. "She might not come with us willingly." The words feel heavy as I admit to my brothers the truth.

Lily thinks of me as the enemy now and I don't blame her. She has every right not to trust me. I lied to her from the moment I met her.

"Then we come up with an alternative plan," Alessio states.

Chapter 21

LILY

I breathe in and out, telling myself I can do this over and over again. I will not fail my family again. I push off my chair and fix my gown. Smoothing it down while looking over any wrinkles I may have created when I sat down.

I look back in the mirror to get a full view of my outfit and I'm pleased with how everything came out in such a short amount of time.

My eyes look glassy from unshed tears and I instantly regret not wearing a veil.

I hear the door beside me open and I see shadow of a man in a suit in my periphery.

I turn expecting to see Enzo returning to get me but to my shock I find Nico standing in front of me.

"What are you doing here?"

Nico takes a step towards me and I back up only to hit the chair and stumble back. Nico grabs hold of my arm and steadies me from falling. The heat from his hand burns me through my lace sleeve on to my skin.

"We need to go. We don't have much time."

I am trying to listen to what he is saying but I can't focus with all the blood rushing to my ears in anger and pain. "Go where?"

Nico pulls on my arm and towards the door, "I am getting you out of here."

I pull out of his grasp and back away. "No, I am not going anywhere with you."

Nico turns to me. "We don't have time for this." I can tell he is losing patience with me but to hell with him.

"I am going to marry Ronan and unless you want to die then you should leave." I cross my arms against my chest in hopes it will give the impression I have made my decision. But in reality it's to hide my shaking hands from Nico's sudden appearance.

I pray he leaves before anyone catches him. I don't want his blood on my hands. And considering the things Ronan has done to me and his own nephew, I can't imagine what he would do to his enemy. The thought sends a cold shiver down my spine, but I try and stay firm.

Nico looks down at me in almost defeat, "I was hoping I wouldn't have to do this."

I furrow my brows in confusion and before I can respond Nico takes a step forward and wraps an arm around me. I am about to protest when I feel something prick the side of my neck.

I place my hand to the spot on my neck, but the room begins to tilt. My hand feels heavy and slumps down next to my body which is also slowly giving in. I slump against Nico's body who wraps an arm around me.

Nico picks me up and carries me in his arms. I want to tell him to stop and put me down but my tongue feels heavy in my mouth.

Nico pulls me further up against his chest as my head lolls on his shoulder. I hear rustling but can't move or look up.

He drugged me. Nico drugged me.

My chest constraints in pain and the tears I have been pushing

KIARA MORGAN

away all day finally flow down my cheek.

Chapter 22

LILY

I wake up in the back of an SUV with a throbbing headache.

I think I am in the back with Nico, but I can't be sure. Considering my head is on someone's lap I hope it's Nico's and not some random person.

From my vantage point I can see two other men at the front. One is driving and another in the passenger seat.

Both have dark hair and are wearing suits, but I don't recognize them. If I had a better view of their faces, maybe then I might be able too. Or maybe not.

I doubt they are my papa's men or someone I would know. It has to be the Vitales.

I can't move my body but can slightly move my fingers, which won't help me much right now.

We hit a pothole and I jerk up and hit my head down on whoever's lap it's on, causing me to moan in pain.

"Shit, she's waking up." I recognize Nico's voice from above me. The slight relief at knowing it's Nico's lap I have my head on is squashed when I remember he drugged and kidnapped me.

"You should have given her a higher dosage," says someone whose voice I don't recognize.

"I didn't want to risk it with the baby," Nico says.

We hit another pothole and again my head flies a few inches up before hitting Nico's lap again. The throbbing headache intensifies each time when my head makes contact with Nico's lap. I whimper in pain each time.

"Fucks sake Carter, can't you drive a bit slower?" Nico seethes before leaning down and kissing my forehead. The throbbing pain dulls for a second at the contact of Nico's lips on my skin.

"I'm trying but we need to get the fuck out of here before Ronan or the Mancini's find out we took Lily."

With the mention of my family's name, the pain comes back in full blast. My eyes well up at the thought of them looking for me. My papa will be furious at someone taking his daughter and destroying his alliance. But it's my brother Enzo I worry about. He will come for me. I know it.

With some movement in my hands, I push my nails into Nico's thighs and try to push myself up but my head feels like a ton of bricks.

Nico wraps his hand around mine and pulls my hand away from his thigh with little resistance. Tears fall down my cheek at how pathetic I really am.

Nico gently kisses the inside of my wrist. "It's going to be okay." His voice is soft and soothing. But I know better now. It's all an act.

The SUV swerves to the side and then the light from the sun disappears. We are somewhere underground. A few seconds later, it halts with a loud screech.

A door opens and I am being pulled out and into Nico's arms again. I try to look over Nico's shoulder to try and get an idea of where we are but all I can see is we are in an underground parking garage.

I hear a ding and then we are inside an elevator before we arrive in an apartment or should say more like a penthouse.

I try and look around for any possible people around I can call for help but see no one in sight.

Inside I get small glimpses of a penthouse and from the view from the window, we are somewhere high.

Nico steps up some stairs that takes us to a second floor in the penthouse before arriving to a bedroom. He gently lays me on a bed and removes my heels.

Nico caresses my hand in his large one. "I'll be right downstairs if you need anything." He looks at me with a look I can't decipher. "I'll be right back."

He places my hand on top of my stomach before rising to his feet and heading to the door.

Nico takes a glance back over his shoulder at me and I use little movement I have to turn my face to the ceiling. A few seconds later I hear the door shut.

NICO

I hated drugging Lily, but I didn't have a choice. She wouldn't have come willingly with me. Not that I blamed her. But the look of betrayal on her beautiful face felt like a stab in the chest.

I get downstairs to the living room and find my brother Carter sitting on the couch.

I look around the apartment. "Where's Alessio?"

"He headed upstairs to his place. He needs to make some calls to make sure we are prepared for any attacks from Ronan or the Mancinis."

They are going to attack. Maybe not Ronan considering he is a piece a shit and will probably find another family to form an alliance with, but the Mancinis will.

We took the Capo's daughter. This is considered an act of war. But I don't regret my actions one bit. As long as I have Lily.

"Can you grab some clothes from Anna for Lily to borrow?" I ask Carter.

Carter raises to his feet. "Sure, I'll also stop by the store and grab some toiletry items Lily might need as well."

"Thanks."

Carter smirks. "Don't thank me. I just want to be out of here before Lily fully wakes up." As if in on cue, we hear a something shatter from upstairs. "I guess she's up."

As Carter heads towards the elevators, I make my way back upstairs.

Chapter 23

LILY

Stupid lamp. The drug has been wearing off me slowly and I'm able to move my arms and sit up slowly but my legs are still numbed.

I tried to pull myself up by grabbing the lamp by the bed but all I ended up doing was falling on my face with the lamp crashing to the ground.

The door opens just as I'm able to push myself up to my elbows; a shadow falls over me. I peer up from underneath my lashes and see Nico standing in front of me.

Damn that bastard.

He crouches down. "Here, let me help you up." He grabs my arm in an effort to help me, but I pull away from him so hard my arm could have popped off my shoulder.

Nico studies my face before sighing and straightening to his full height. "I was only trying to help."

Help. Drugging and kidnapping me is helping. Destroying my family is helping. If that is what he considers help, I don't want it.

I use all the force I can muster up and push myself into a sitting position. Having used up my energy, I lean back against the bed for support.

Nico grabs a chair from the corner of the room and drags it near the bed and takes a seat. "I know you're mad and maybe even hate me. But I need you to listen to me."

I turn away from Nico and stare at the wall in front of me. I don't want to hear anything he has to say. I don't need to hear any more lies. Every time he speaks or tries to explain I feel like my heart is being ripped apart over and over again.

"When I first approached you, I told myself I needed to get closer to you to get to Ronan. But after a while it stopped being about Ronan. You might not believe me, but I've fallen in love with you."

His words burn through my soul. He says he loves me and the stupid part of me wants to believe it. For once someone loves me.

"You might not believe me, and it might not seem like it but I'm doing this for us and our baby."

"Stop," I croak. I can't hear it anymore.

"No, I need you to know. I know I am being selfish but I don't care. I love you Lily and you are mine. Mine only. Not Ronan's. Not anyone else's. Mine."

I turn and finally face him and his gaze burns into me my heart. *Don't fall for it, Lily.*

I turn away from him before I stupidly believe his lies. "Go away," I force out despite the way my throat is tightening with pain.

Nico nods. "I'll be downstairs if you need anything."

"What I need is to go back to family! What I need is to get married!" I shout in anger. A tear slips down my cheek despite my resistance to stop any from coming out.

Nico rises to his feet. "You are not getting married, and you are not leaving."

Nico pushes the chair back into the corner and grabs the fallen lamp pieces from the ground and leaves with it.

VENGEFUL PRINCE

Once the door closes shut, the remaining tears I have been forcing down finally fall endlessly once I am alone.

Chapter 24

LILY

After an hour, I finally got feeling back in my legs. I walk over to the window and look out. The skyline looks beautiful up here. Nico mentioned his penthouse had a better view then the Empire State Building and he wasn't lying.

I consider making a run for it now that I am fully able use my legs but hesitate, wondering who else might be here.

Nico had mentioned he would be downstairs, but he kidnapped me with two other men. For all I know they are still here and could be a threat.

I want to think Nico would never hurt me but the Nico I knew was a lie. He was playing me. Using me.

I blink away the stupid tears that form again.

I can't keep sitting here crying. I need to get out of here and get back to my family.

Someone knocks on the door and I jump at the sudden noise. I know it's not Nico. He wouldn't knock. He didn't even knock at my apartment, and I doubt he would in his own place.

I don't answer the door. Partly due to anger but also out of fear.

The door slightly opens and a man with dark hair and brown eyes walks in with a bag. "I brought you some clothes and other things you might need." He places the bag on the bed. "Is there anything else you need?"

"I need to get out of here."

He smirks. "That I can't help you with."

I knew he wouldn't help me, but I thought I give it a try anyways. "Who are you?"

"Carter. I'm Nico's younger brother."

I've heard of Nico's older brother and Capo of the Vitale family but not much else about the rest of the family. I look closely at Carter and realize he and Nico look quite alike. They have similar bone structure and coloring.

"Where is Nico?" I ask.

"Downstairs. He thought you wouldn't want to see him right now."

He's right. I don't want to see him.

"If you want, I can go get him," Carter offers.

"No," I say too quickly. "I just want to be left alone."

Carter nods in understanding before turning away and heading towards the door. "If you need anything, let me know."

"Thanks," I say but regret immediately. I shouldn't be thanking the people kidnapping me for anything.

Carter doesn't say anything but just nods before walking out and closing the door behind him.

I head to the bed and look through the bag. There is a couple of outfits and I pick out a pair of leggings, shirt and flats. Needing an outfit that I can run in rather then my puffy lace wedding dress that would only slow me down.

After I change, I head towards the door to sneak out and find an exit.

I go to open the door and to my shock it doesn't open. It's locked.

They locked me in here!

I laugh like a crazy woman at myself and my situation.

Of course, they would lock me in here. They are the enemy and they kidnapped me. I am not here by choice.

I turn and look around the room. I need to find something that can help me escape or worse case use as a weapon. I don't want to hurt anyone but for all I know they could be planning on hurting me.

There is a dresser across the room. I pull the first drawer open only to find it empty. I continue opening up the remaining drawers and they are all empty.

I walk over to the bedside tables and find those drawers empty as well.

Aside from the bed, empty drawers, the chair in the corner, and the bag Carter brought me, there is nothing in this room I can use as a weapon. I might have been able to the use the lamp I dropped earlier but Nico took that with him when he left.

There is a door leading to a bathroom across the room. I run in there hoping to find a weapon but like the bedroom, it's completely bare. The only thing I could find is a roll of toilet paper and I can't see myself using that as a weapon of any sorts.

I slam the bathroom drawers back shut hard out of frustration and slump down against the wall. I am truly and utterly screwed.

NICO

I just made myself a drink when the elevator dings open. Alessio walks into Carter's penthouse that I am currently occupying with my kidnapped love.

Alessio looks at the drink in my hand. "Now is not really the best time to be drinking."

I swirl the amber liquid in my glass. After the look of hate Lily gave me, I needed a drink. "Is something wrong?"

"Aside from us kidnapping Lorenzo Mancini's daughter and declaring war with them?"

I finally ask the question I am afraid to know the answer to. "Do they know we have Lily?"

Alessio takes a deep breathe. "Yeah, they do. They think we took Lily for retaliation for Ronan taking Anna."

That was the plan before I got close to Lily. Take her to hurt Ronan the way he hurt Alessio.

Carter walks into the room. "What's going on?"

Alessio faces me. "Lorenzo wants to make a deal. He contacted me and asked for Lily back."

"No fucking way! They are not getting Lily back no matter what," I declare. I'm not letting Lily go, no matter what. Even if I have to go against my own brothers. The thought of fighting my brothers sickens me but I can't lose Lily or my baby.

Alessio nods. "I will try and buy us time by stretching out negotiations but if Lily doesn't want to be here, we can't keep her locked up forever."

Alessio is right. We can fight the Mancinis all we want but if Lily doesn't want to be with me, I can't stop her forever.

"I just need some time." Time to convince Lily to forgive me.

Chapter 25

LILY

I feel like I am losing my mind. I have been pacing around this room for hours trying to come up with a plan. But so far I've come up with nothing. The sun has set and it's night now.

I wonder what my family is doing or thinking. Do they know I'm here? Are they worried about me?

The door screeches open, bringing me out of my thoughts. I look up to see Nico standing near the door with a tray of food in his hands.

He places the food on the bed. "I thought you might be hungry."

I have the urge to toss the food at him, but I am hungry. I barely ate this morning from jitters about my wedding day.

Nico places his hands in his dress pants. "You should eat for the baby at least."

"If you cared about the baby, you would have let me just get married! I had a plan and you ruined everything!" I shout in irritation. As much as I hated marrying that monster Ronan, it was the only way to fix the mess I'm in.

Nico raises his eyebrow in question. "How would marrying Ronan benefit the baby?"

I close my mouth shut. I can't tell him my plan.

Nico's face changes from questioning to deadly anger. This is the Nico that I feared. The Nico that he kept hidden away from me as he played me like a fiddle.

Nico takes steps towards me. "I asked you a question Lily. How would marrying Ronan help our baby?"

As he advances towards me, I back up in alarm only to hit the dresser against the wall.

"Answer me." His voice calm but his eyes are saying something else.

Nico's gaze feels like it could burn a hole in my face, so I look away and stare down at the wooden floors to avoid his stare.

Nico grabs my chin with his hand and nudges it up towards him. His touch is gentle and full of heat.

"I'm going to ask one last time, what does marrying Ronan have to do with our baby?" I hear the threat in his voice.

"I-I was going to tell Ronan it was his baby," I stammer out. Not the most genius plan but that was all I had. Let Ronan think I got pregnant by him and hope he thinks I just went into early labour when I gave birth.

Nico's eyes shift into a fury I've never seen. I get the impulse to back away again, but I am trapped between the dresser and his body. I try and slide sideways, but he slams his hand down on the dresser trapping me. I flinch back at his reaction, hitting my back against the dresser.

Nico looks down at me with an unreadable expression before taking a step back from me. I slide to the side and push up against the wall putting further space between us.

I force my gaze down and wait. Not sure for what but I'm assuming his anger or even worse.

After a few seconds I hear the door shut and I look up to see Nico is gone.

NICO

I stomp down the stairs in anger and head straight towards the elevator.

"Where are you going?" I hear Carter say from behind me.

I don't respond. I can't respond to him. If I do, I might just lose it. All I can think about is how Lily planned on passing my child off as Ronan's. That and she planned on fucking him.

I don't know what is causing me anger more, my child being raised by Ronan or his hands on Lily. My Lily.

I am in the parking garage making my way to my car to get as far away as possible to cool down when Gia blocks my path.

"I've been trying to get in contact with you for hours."

"Fuck off, Gia." I don't have time for her bullshit. I walk around her and open my car down when Gia slams it shut.

"I want my credit cards now! If you don't, I will tell everyone you're an abusive asshole," she says smugly with a smile.

"Go ahead," I seethe out through gritted teeth. I don't care what the fuck she does or what people think. In our line of work people tend to think the worst of you already.

Gia drops her smile. "Give me my credit cards or I will have my brother pay a visit to your damn whore you kept hidden and have a bullet put through her head. Maybe he'll fuck her before he puts her out of her misery."

All I see is red when I grab Gia by the neck and push her up against my car. "Or maybe I'll put a bullet through your head instead."

Gia kicks at my legs in an attempt to get me to release her but I have the urge to let the dumb bitch die by strangulation.

"Nico, let her go!" Carter shouts from across the parking garage as he runs towards us.

I look down at Gia as she tries to gasp for air and as much as I hate her, killing her won't solve the problem. I already have a shit ton of problems and don't need this on top of it.

I loosen my grip around Gia's neck and toss her to the side. She falls on her hands and knees to the ground while coughing for air.

Carter is beside me now. "Are you okay?"

"I need to get the fuck out of here," I say to Carter.

"Okay, I'll take care of things here."

I get in my car and speed out of the garage as fast possible.

I've been at the gym for hours trying to release all my anger out. First I tried by hitting the punching bag until I exhausted myself but that did nothing. Then I tried fighting some of the other soldiers practicing at the family gym. Some of landed a few good punches but that only made the anger boil within me more.

After knocking out the sixth soldier, the others refused to fight me. Which only angered me more.

I look at the clock and it's nearing midnight. I grab my phone and text Carter.

How are things back at the penthouse?

Carter responds a few seconds later.

Fine. Lily fell asleep about 2 hours ago.

I pack up and head back to the penthouse. Once I arrive, I make my way to Carter's spare bedroom I've been using for the last couple of years. I toss my gym bag to the side and take a cold shower. Even the cold water couldn't cool me down.

After changing into a pair of sweatpants, I head to Lily's room. I unlock the door and walk in.

She is fast asleep. I can't help but run the back of my index finger against her soft cheeks.

Lily feared me. I saw the look on her face. She thought I was going to hit her. I would never hit her. No matter how angry I got I would never touch a hair on her head. She doesn't realize how much she means to me.

I pull the cover down and get into bed with her. Once I'm settled in, I pull Lily towards me. She shifts in her sleep but then settles quickly.

Her soft breathing against my chest soothes the remaining anger I had. I run my hand down her soft brown hair and kiss the top of crown.

I don't blame her for any of this. It's my fault. She was going to marry Ronan because that is what she thought she had to do to protect our baby and her family. She didn't think she had any other option. I pushed her into making that decision.

I will never let her feel that way again.

Chapter 26

LILY

I wake up to a warm embrace. I tilt my head up and see Nico. I feel like I am in some sort of dream. Slowly the haze starts to wear off and I remember Nico kidnapped me. I jerk up and away from Nico.

Nico groans, "What time is it?" He grabs his phone from the bedside table and looks at the time on the screen. "It's 5am. Go back to sleep, Lily."

Realising I lost an opportunity there to grab Nico's phone, I internally yell at myself for being stupid once again.

"Lily, please go back to sleep," Nico pleads in his sleep state.

I slowly lean back down on the bed. Maybe if he falls back asleep, I can grab his phone. As soon as I lay back down on to the bed, Nico pulls me back towards him. I feel rigid in his grasp, not knowing how to handle this situation.

I can feel his heartbeat beneath my cheek and his warm body against mine. Being in Nico's hold brings back memories and feelings I want to forget. With them is the pain and heartache from the betrayal.

After a while I look up at Nico to see if he is asleep. I slowly pull out from his grasp and wait. He looks like he is asleep, but this could be an act. I look to the side and see his phone laying on the bedside table.

I slowly get out of bed and circle around the bed. My heart feels like it's being pushed against my ribs as I slowly pick up Nico's phone. I keep expecting him to open his eyes and catch me.

After standing in the same spot next to the bed with the phone in my hand for a few seconds I slowly back away.

I'm near the bathroom when my foot lands on a creak. I freeze at the sudden noise and look towards the bed.

I take another step back and another creak, louder this time, is made. Nico rustles in bed and looks to his side. *Shit, he's awake.*

I quickly run to the bathroom before he realizes I have his phone and lock the door behind me.

"Lily!" Nico bellows from the other side of the door. "Open the door now!"

My hands are shaking as I turn on his phone. Shit he has a passcode on his phone. I consider a million options in my head in a span of a few seconds what his passcode be, from 1234 to his birth date. I type in his birth date and it's wrong. *Shit.*

"Lily." This time Nico's voice is calm. That scares me even more. "You have five seconds to open the door."

I decide to try my birth date and to my shock the phone unlocks. My birth date was Nico's passcode.

Nico starts counting down. "1…. 2….."

With shaky hands, I dial my brother's number. At first, I press the wrong button and have to go back and dial again.

I hear the phone start ringing just as Nico gets to 5.

He has gone completely silent and all I can hear is the ringing from the phone.

Enzo picks up. "Hello?"

Before I can speak a loud thud is heard before the door goes flying off its hinges and shatters into wooden pieces in every direction.

I scream at the sudden burst and Nico walks into the bathroom as if he didn't just break down the door into a million pieces.

"Lily, is that you?" I hear my brother say from the other side of the phone line. I can't respond and can only stayed glued in place like a statue.

"Lily, don't worry, I'm going to come for you," my brother says.

Nico grabs the phone out of my hand and looks down at it before hanging up the call. He looks at me with the same fury he had yesterday until all of a sudden something shifts.

"I'm going to go grab breakfast." Nico turns around and walks out of the bathroom.

Leaving me utterly confused.

NICO

I head downstairs to the kitchen and find Carter sitting on a stool at the kitchen island in nothing but boxers, drinking coffee and reading the New York Times.

He looks up at me. "I'm to assume that was you a few minutes ago and not a bomb going off?"

"Fuck off," I murmur.

Carter puts down the newspaper. "What happened?"

"I was stupid and left my phone in plain sight for Lily to get too." I walk towards the fridge and pull out some eggs and place them on the counter.

"That doesn't sound like you. You usually wouldn't make a mistake like that."

He's right I wouldn't but Lily has a way of making me put my guard down around her.

I pull out the pan and set it on the stove. "Do you want eggs? I'm making some for Lily."

"I'm good. I actually have some things I need to take care of so I should be heading to work." Carter pushes off the stool and walks out of the kitchen.

I make scrambled eggs and cut some fruit and take it upstairs on a tray with orange juice.

When I enter the room Lily's in, I find her sitting on the bed and her head flies in my direction as soon as I walk in.

She slowly rises from her bed and I can see the hesitation in her eyes.

I place the tray on the bed. "You're going to have to eat in here until I know you won't try to run away or try and contact your family again."

Lily peers up at me from beneath her long lashes. "You're not mad?"

I sigh. "No, it's my fault. I should have known you would have tried to contact your family. I let my guard down. It's my fault."

Lily bites on her lower lip and slowly nods but I can tell she doesn't believe me when I tell her I'm not mad. The only person I'm mad at is myself.

"I can't get someone to come in and fix the door so you're going to have to make do like that," I tell Lily.

Her emerald eyes widen. "How do you expect me to use the bathroom with the door wide open?"

I shrug. "I did tell you to open the door. You didn't listen so I had to break it down. Now you're going to have to live with it."

"For how long?"

I don't know how to answer Lily. Not sure if she's asking about the door or how long she is meant to stay here. I don't have answers for either. I didn't exactly plan this through.

"Eat, I'll be back later. There are some things I have to take care of." I nudge the tray towards her direction, but she doesn't move from her spot.

Maybe giving her some space might help. I turn towards the door and leave, locking the door behind me. As much as I hate locking Lily in, I need to make sure she doesn't try anything again.

I head to my room and take a shower and change. I need to let Alessio know Lily contacted her family. She may have not got the chance to tell them anything important, but he needs to be aware of it in case they try and contact him.

After taking a shower and changing, I take the private elevator to Alessio's floor and walk into his living room. Alessio's daughter Emma is sitting on the couch watching a ballet performance.

Emma has seems to have grown obsessed with ballet lately.

She turns in my direction and gives me a large smile. "Did you come to see Daddy?"

I pick Emma up into my arms. "No, I came to see you."

Her smile widens further. "Really?"

"Really."

Anna walks into the room with Daniele in her arms. "Nico, what a surprise to see you. Did you want me to have Greta make you something for breakfast?" she offers.

I place Emma back down on the couch. "No, I'm fine. Where is Alessio?"

"Alessio is in his office." Daniele tugs on Anna's light blonde hair and she looks down at him with a frown. Daniele on the other hand gives a toothless smile to his mom.

Seeing my niece and nephew, I can't help but wonder about my baby. Will it be a girl or a boy? Will my child look like me or Lily?

Anna looks at me. "Is everything okay?" I can see the concern on her face.

I give her a reassuring smile. "Everything is fine."

Anna doesn't need to know what is going on. She has suffered enough because of Ronan.

Emma tugs on my suit jacket. "You promised me you would play with me. Let's play now."

"Emma, your uncle is very busy," Anna reprimands Emma.

Emma in turn gives Anna a pout.

I squat down to Emma's eye level. "I'll play with you later once I'm done speaking with your dad."

Emma smiles. "Okay."

I straighten and head towards Alessio's office. I don't bother knocking and enter.

Alessio is sitting at his desk with a number of files and looks up at me when I walk in.

He rises to his feet and crosses his arms. "Do you want to explain to me what happened with Gia?"

Fuck, I forgot about her. "She had it coming."

"Her father called me and informed me Gia called him in a hysterical fit claiming you beat her up."

I roll my eyes. "That is an overstatement." Putting my hands on Gia wasn't right but she provoked me. "What did you tell her father?" I already know Alessio put him in his place. He hates others interfering in his family's private business.

"That he should worry more about his and his son's lack of work instead of Gia's bullshit."

I knew my brother would have my back.

Alessio continues, "Are you going to tell me what happened?"

I take a seat on the couch at the side of Alessio's office, needing to sit for this conversation. Every time I think about it, I feel like I am about to burst from all the anger. "Lily told me she planned on marrying Ronan and pretending the baby was his."

"Makes sense now why the sudden change of the wedding date. The sooner she got married, the less far along the pregnancy she would have been. Easier to pull off the lie."

"I was so angry at finding out Lily planned on having my child with Ronan and letting him touch her, I lost it when I ran into Gia. She kept pushing my buttons until I couldn't take it anymore."

Alessio rounds his desk and comes to sit on the couch next to me. "Nico, this shit has become a huge mess. The Mancinis are threatening to attack our territory if we don't return Lily to them."

"What about Ronan?" I bet the fucker is probably pissed we took his bride.

"Surprisingly quiet. He hasn't made an attempt to contact us and almost seems like he doesn't care. To him Lily was just a way to build an alliance with the Mancini family. I doubt he cared for her or is worried for her well-being. He is probably already on the hunt for a new family he can make an alliance with now that we have Lily. Unless he is waiting for Lily to be returned so he can try again."

"He is not getting Lily," I state in anger. "I just need some time for her to be more accepting of the situation."

Alessio raises an eyebrow. "Situation? That is putting it lightly. Dishonoring her and the Mancinis by having a child out of wedlock, going to war with her family and possibly killing the people she loves."

I don't want to kill her family, but we might not have a choice, especially if they attack. After that, Lily will for sure never forgive me.

"Speaking of her family, there is something you should know. Lily got her hands on my phone while I was sleeping and called her brother. The call didn't last more than a few seconds and she wasn't able to say anything to him, but I thought you should know."

I can tell from Alessio's face he is wondering the same thing Carter was this morning. How the fuck I let my guard down. But he doesn't ask.

"I will let you know if her brother or anyone from her family contacts us. But Nico, you need to be prepared."

Prepared to make a choice.

Chapter 27

LILY

I ate the food Nico brought me. I could tell he made it himself. Each bite I took, I was reminded of my traitorous actions. As the food went down my throat, it felt heavy as it sat in my stomach. I eventually had to hurl it all out.

I'm assuming it has to do with my pregnancy more than anything.

I feel nauseous and sick as I lay down on the marble floors in the bathroom next to the toilet. I tried to get up before but within seconds I had to run back to let out more of the contents I ate.

After the third time, I gave up and just decided to lay next to the toilet to have quick and easy access.

The cool marble floors feel nice against my hot and sweaty face. The broken pieces of wood from the door are still scattered all over the place.

Nico said he wasn't mad, and I believe him. He genuinely seemed like he blamed himself. I almost felt guilty for a second but then I reminded myself he is to blame.

I hear the wood pieces crack under someone's weight, and I shoot my eyes open. I see Nico's dress pants and shoes standing in front of me but don't have the energy to look up.

Nico crouches down and places a hand on my cheek. "Lily, is something wrong?"

I close my eyes at his touch. Trying to push away the memories of how gentle and kind they could be. After taking a heavy breath I answer, "Fine, I just feel nauseous."

Nico loops his hands under my body and pulls me towards him before picking me up. He carries me to the bedroom and places me on the bed before pulling the blanket up to my chest.

"I'll call a doctor." He almost sounds concerned. Maybe he is.

Concerned his leverage to Ronan might die. *Or maybe for you because he does care.* I push that stupid thought away.

Nico pulls out his phone from his pant pocket and texts something. "The doctor will be here shortly. Do you need anything?"

I feel a bubble of a laugh forming in my throat. I need a lot of things, but I know he means for the nausea. "No. Just rest."

Nico kneels down and kisses my temple before straightening. "I'll be back once the doctor arrives. Rest until then."

Once Nico is gone and the door is closed, I close my eyes to rest.

I'm woken by Nico hovering over me.

"Lily, the doctor is here to see you." He helps me up. "The doctor is going to see you downstairs."

"I'm allowed to leave the room?"

Nico frowns. "Don't try anything. I just didn't want the doctor to see you locked up in here with the pieces of wood all over the place."

I look around the room and it does look like a mess for a room with so little furniture.

Nico holds me by the elbow as I push to my feet and get out of bed. Nico pulls me by my wrist towards the hallway and I try and pull out of his grasp, but he doesn't let go my wrist.

Downstairs in the living is a man waiting who looks to be probably in his mid-fifties.

He gives me a kind smile. "Hello. I am Dr. Watson. I hear you have not been feeling well. Why don't you take a seat on the couch?"

I lick my lips and consider if I should tell the kind doctor I've been kidnapped and held against my will. Maybe he will help.

"Don't bother, he works for the family," Nico says. I startle at the fact that he knew what I was thinking before I even did anything.

I walk over to the couch and take a seat as the doctor takes out a number of items from his bag.

Looking around the living room, you can tell a man lives here. It's all blue and grey but still stylish.

The doctor takes out a needle. "I just need to take some blood to test the sample."

I roll up my shirt sleeve to give the doctor better access. He is quick but gentle and is done within seconds.

The doctor places the sample in his bag before turning to me. "Nico mentioned you are a month along in your pregnancy. Have you taken any sort of prenatal vitamins or seen a doctor besides the initial visit to the ER?"

I'm thrown off at the doctor knowing about me being pregnant and my visit to the ER. I glare up at Nico who seems to show no emotion or reaction whatsoever. It won't be long before word starts to spread and gets back to my family. My family who is probably at war for me.

I turn back to the doctor to respond. "No."

The doctor takes out a notepad and writes down something. "I will have a list of vitamins you should start taking and you need to book an appointment with an obstetrician." He rips the piece of paper from his notepad and hands it to Nico who takes it without a second thought.

"If you need anything else, call me," the doctor tells Nico before packing up and heading for the elevator.

Once the doctor is gone, I'm expecting Nico to take me back upstairs but he doesn't. Instead, he turns on the television and takes a seat next to me on the couch. "Do you want to watch something? I recorded some of your favorite shows in case you missed an episode."

He goes through a list of shows that are recorded. Shows I like. A ball of pain in my chest begins to form and my eyes well up.

I can't take this anymore. "Why are you doing this?" I rasp out as tears fall freely down my cheeks.

Nico looks surprised by my reaction. "I thought you would enjoy watching your shows."

"No," I cry. "Why are you doing this. Pretending. Playing with my mind. Stop it!" I shout the last two words. My body starts to tremble as I feel the walls I built up the last few days slowly crumbling around me.

"Lily," Nico starts, "I'm not pretending or playing with you. I love…"

"Don't say it!" I cut Nico off and rise to my feet. "Stop lying! You said it yourself I was just a way to get to Ronan. Well, you have me so stop it!"

I can't see Nico's face anymore now because my eyes are blurry with tears.

Nico stands up and walks towards me. "I am not lying. I do love you. What is it going to take for you to believe that?"

I place my arm out to block him from coming closer. "Let me go." I don't know how that proves anything, but I just need to be far away from him as possible.

"No," he says firmly.

The remaining mental wall I had made crashes down in finality. He is not going to let me go ever.

Nico closes the distance between us and pulls me towards him in an embrace as I cry into his chest. "I can't let you go, Lily. I'm sorry." His voice is soft yet apologetic.

Chapter 28

LILY

I wake up and look around at my surroundings. This room is different from the one I was in previously. I climb out of bed and walk over to the window and pull the curtains. It's dark outside.

After crying my eyes out, I had exhausted myself mentally and physically. Nico carried me upstairs to bed. I had assumed it was the same room as before but he must have brought me to another.

Despite sleeping for a couple hours, I still feel exhausted.

Not sure if it's the pregnancy or the emotional rollercoaster I've been on for the last several days. But it's starting to take a toll on me.

My stomach growls and I place my hand on my stomach. I ate this morning but threw up almost all of what I ate and more this morning.

I walk over to the door expecting for it to be locked as usual, but when I turn the handle, it opens.

I stand in the middle of the doorframe trying to figure out if Nico forgot to lock the door by accident or if I'm even allowed to leave.

When my stomach growls again, I decide to risk it for food and leave the room.

Once I get downstairs, I'm in the living room where I previously had met the kind doctor.

I'm about to turn left when I notice the elevator to my right.

I head to the elevator and push the button to call it up. As soon as I hit the button a passcode option pops up from the screen above the button. Damn it. I knew it was too easy.

I input my birthdate hoping it's the same passcode as Nico's phone. The passcode is incorrect, so I try Nico's birthdate this time. Again incorrect. I decide to input a random combination and due to a third incorrect attempt, the screen locks.

I'm fidgeting with the screen to unlock it when I hear a voice behind me. "Don't bother. You won't figure out the combination."

I twirl suddenly towards the voice and see Carter standing behind me.

"How long have you been standing there?" I ask with my hand on my chest.

"Not long, I got a notification someone was trying to enter a passcode on my phone."

I take in this new information. "So, you didn't lock me in the bedroom because I am technically locked in this penthouse."

"No, we didn't lock you in the bedroom because Nico thought you would like to be able to roam around freely."

I purse my lips. "Freely?"

Carter crosses his arms against his chest. "Would you rather be locked up in the bedroom again?"

"Is that a threat?"

"Just trying to get you to see the brighter side of things. Dinner is ready in the kitchen if you're hungry." Carter turns around and walks down a hallway.

Considering my growling my stomach, I decide to follow him. It's not like I can escape from the elevator.

Once I round the corner and walk into the kitchen, my nose is in heaven. I smell chicken parmesan and the scent is too much for my stomach. It's doing cartwheels from just the smell alone.

Carter grabs a plate and fills it up with food and slides it across the counter towards me.

I grab it instantly without thinking, needing to fill my stomach.

After filling himself up a plate and taking a seat at the table, I follow him and sit across from him.

We eat in silence at first but needing to end the awkwardness, I decide to ask questions. "Where's Nico?"

"He had to deal with some things."

"Does it involve me or my family?"

Carter doesn't respond this time. All of a sudden, the food feels heavy in my stomach again. My family probably thinks I'm being tortured and here I am eating with the enemy at his kitchen table.

I glance around the kitchen and don't see any phones or computers. There could be one in another room.

Using this chance at Nico not being here and being allowed privilege to roam around, I rise from my chair. "I'm done eating. I think I'm just going to watch a movie or something."

Carter nods. "Sure, do whatever you want."

I take my dishes to the sink and make my way back to the living room. After doing a quick search, I find nothing of use to me. Thinking maybe they hid them, I decide to look under the furniture.

I'm on my hands and knees looking under the coffee table when I hear Carter. "The remote is on top of the table not underneath."

I hit my head on the underside of the table from Carter's sudden appearance with a loud thud.

I crawl out from under the table and rub the top of my head to soothe the pain.

Carter walks over to the coffee table and hands me the remote. "You're not going to find anything. Just watch a movie or something instead."

I rip the remote out of his hand in annoyance and turn on the TV.

"I'll be upstairs in my room if you need anything," Carter says as he walks up the stairs.

"I won't," I murmur more to myself.

After I'm sure Carter is upstairs, I continue my search of the room. When I don't find anything, I go back into the kitchen and search there.

Weirdly enough some of the drawers were locked. I felt like a baby trying to unlock a baby proof lock. After jiggling around the drawer to get it to open for a few minutes, I give up and decide to look at the other rooms.

I find a game room with a pool table and a bar but find nothing of use in there either.

After looking through all the rooms downstairs, I consider checking the ones upstairs but decide against it.

Not knowing which room Carter's in, it would be risky for me to open random doors.

I settle back on the couch and put on one the shows Nico recorded earlier.

As I'm watching the show, all I can think about is how Nico put in the effort to record them.

I keep replaying his words earlier in my head. That he loves me.

I'm clearly not a great judge of character, but I badly want to believe him.

That it wasn't just all in my head. That he truly cares and loves me, the way I do for him.

I hear the elevator behind me open and I turn around and see Nico walk in.

When his gaze settles on me, he gives me that handsome smile that makes me melt and walks towards me.

He leans down and kiss the top of my crown. "How are you feeling?"

My heart feels heavy at seeing him and showering me with affection.

"Are you still feeling sick?" Nico's face switches from happy to worry.

I shake my head. "No, I feel better now." My voice comes out quieter than I intended.

Nico smiles and walks around the couch and settles next to me. "What are you watching?"

I turn off the TV considering I can't focus on the show. "I'm actually tired now." I push off the couch and start walking up the stairs. I hear Nico following behind.

I reach the room I was previously locked in and I'm about to walk in when Nico stops me. "Why are you going in there?"

I turn to face him confusion. "Isn't this my room?"

Nico grabs my hand. "Not anymore. You're staying in my room."

He pulls me to the unknown room I woke up in earlier.

"This is your room?"

Nico nods. "I'm just going to shower and change. You can go to sleep if you're tired."

Nico walks over to the bathroom and once I hear the shower turn on, I decide to rummage through his drawers. Considering this is Nico's room, there must be a phone or laptop around here somewhere.

After searching through his entire belongings, I come out empty handed once again. Nico must have hidden everything. Which would explain why I'm allowed to wander around freely all of a sudden.

I crawl into bed and close my eyes to try and sleep when a thought passes through me.

I sit up and fling off the comforter and walk to the walk in closet. The entire closet is lined up with clothes and shoes. Only a man's.

I hear the bathroom door open, and Nico walks out with only black boxers on.

Nico raises an eyebrow and I realize I have been gawking at him for longer than I should.

Feeling my face go red, I turn away from him and back at the closet. "This isn't your room, is it?"

"Of course it is."

"Then where is your wife clothes," I point out.

Something passes over Nico's face before he answers, "She doesn't stay here."

Considering I am sleeping in his bed, I would hope not. "Where does she stay?"

Nico groans. "Let's not talk about this."

"Why not?" I snap. "You are married, aren't you? What does your wife think about you kidnapping your whore and holding her hostage?" Remembering the word she used when she confronted me.

"You are not a whore and don't ever fucking say that again," Nico roars, causing me to flinch. He rubs his eyes with his thumb and forefinger. "I didn't mean to snap at you." His voice is now softer. "I don't want you thinking you're a whore."

"But I am. I slept with a married man."

"You didn't know and I approached you."

How could I forget? He approached me to get to Ronan. "I know now. Which is why we shouldn't be in the same room." I start to walk towards the exit when Nico wraps his arms around my waist and carries me to the bed. "Put me down." I try and kick but end up only hitting air.

Nico places me on the bed. "Stop being silly. Go to sleep."

"You are married!"

Nico gets into bed, and I try and crawl out, but he grabs me by the waist again and pulls me towards him in a hug and lies down, taking me with him.

I try and squirm out of his hold but it's too strong. Having used up my entire stamina, I finally give up.

"You're married. This is wrong." I look up at Nico hoping I can reason with him.

Nico sighs. "I never wanted to marry Gia."

I peer up at him. "What do you mean? Was it arranged?"

"No," Nico laughs. "She was my brother Alessio's first wife's best friend. I hooked up with her one night while I was drunk. A few weeks later she told me she was pregnant." My stomach churns at the thought Nico might have kids and I'm destroying a family. He continues, "Turns out she lied. She was never pregnant. She wanted to marry me for power and money."

"You don't have kids then?" I ask.

"No." His voice filled with sadness. "I can't divorce her either since we are Catholic." I understand what he means. In the mafia you can kill and have affairs, but God forbid you have a divorce. That is considered the biggest sin in the eyes of the mafia.

"So, you stay here and your wife stays somewhere else?"

"This is Carter's place. I've been staying here for the last couple of years."

For some reason the thought that Nico and Gia haven't lived under the same roof fills me with joy and something else. Something I shouldn't be having considering the situation.

I need to figure out how to push these damn feelings and thoughts away. Get them out of my system.

Nico leans over to the bedside table and closes the light. "Go to sleep now, Lily."

I place my head on Nico's warm chest and use it as a pillow as I try and fall asleep.

NICO

I'm woken from my slumber to movement beside me. I already can tell from the strawberry smell, it's Lily.

My heart aches at the thought she is trying to escape again. I made sure to lock away all the electronics and, just in case, any weapons.

There is a slight shift and I consider opening my eyes and letting her know I'm awake but the thought of finding her trying to escape is too much for me. I keep my eyes closed in the hopes she might reconsider.

Suddenly, I feel a soft leg slide across my abs. Then pressure from weight and warmth.

I jerk open my eyes and see Lily straddling me. "What are you doing?"

"Getting something out of my system," she breathes.

Fuck. She pulls her nightie over her head and is now completely naked. She writhes down me until she is directly above my now rock-hard cock.

Through clenched teeth I try and reason with Lily. "We shouldn't be doing this."

Lily furrows her eyebrows. "I know why I shouldn't be, but why not you?"

I'm trying to think of a reason why I shouldn't be, but I can't come up with one besides Lily will regret this later and I don't want to see her in pain again.

Lily grabs my cock out of my boxers and pulls it out. I feel like I'm going to explode in just her hands.

"Lily..." I exhale.

She leans down and licks the top of my head. I feel like my jaw is going to break from how tight I have it pressed together.

"I've never given anyone a blow job before," Lily says as she licks up my shaft all the way to my tip. "But I've seen someone give it before." I'm trying to listen to what she is saying but it's hard to concentrate. "Ronan took me to strip club once and had me watch because he wanted me to learn so I could give him a proper blow job."

He fucking did what?! I'm seeing red, but before I can react or say anything Lily takes me into her mouth. She slowly goes down and then back up while massaging me with her small delicate hands. She starts to speed up and go deeper and I fist her hair around my hand. I feel myself ready to explode

"Lily, I'm going to come," I warn.

She doesn't stop though but instead speeds up further, causing her to choke a number of times from taking me too deep. Fuck. When I can't take it anymore, I release with a jolt going through my body. As I'm coming down, Lily continues to lick and swallow. Lily straightens as she licks the remainder off her lips.

Once I am finally able to get my thoughts together, I grab hold of Lily's waist and flip her over onto her back while I'm above her. She screeches at my sudden movement.

Her eyes widen with shock and terror. I don't like Lily scared but remembering what she told me earlier, I need answers. "Ronan made you watch someone get a blowjob?" I ask with barely restrained anger.

Lily swallows. "No… he had me watch someone give him a blow job." Fuck that's even worse.

"And what did you think?"

She looks unsure at first before answering, "I hated it, but it worked, didn't it?"

I nestle myself between Lily's legs. "So you were thinking of Ronan when you were giving me a blowjob?"

Lily's beautiful emerald eyes widen further but before she can answer, I push into her in one deep thrust. She arches her back from the sudden intrusion and grips my biceps.

"Are you still thinking about Ronan?" I ask as I pull out and slam back into her hard. Her nails dig deeper into me. "I need an answer, Lily." I continue to pull out and slam into her long hard thrusts.

Lily whimpers as her head tilts back before responding, "No."

I can't help the smile that forms on my face as I pull out and slam back into her this time faster.

She withers underneath me before she tightens around me like a vice as she orgasms. I continue thrusting into her until I too follow up with my own release matching her.

I push myself onto my elbows to prevent me from crushing Lily with my body as I catch my breathe.

Lily wiggles under me causing me to go hard once again and her eyes fly open at the sudden change. I kiss her gently on the mouth

VENGEFUL PRINCE

making her melt against my touch before I pull out and thrust back in.

Chapter 29

LILY

My body has never felt this sore. Screwing Nico out of my system was clearly not the answer. Despite multiple rounds, it's still not enough.

He imprinted himself into my heart and soul a long time ago.

Part of me hoped it was only physical but it's more than that. Every time he touched me, I felt my skin flame up from head to toe.

I'm trying to go back to sleep considering it's still dark from being early morning when I feel the contents of my stomach churn and about to come out.

I jump out of bed and run to the washroom at lightning speed as I hurl everything out into the toilet.

Despite having soreness, thankfully I can still move.

"Lily," I hear Nico's voice before he appears in the doorway. "Are you alright?"

I don't get a chance to respond as I hurl another round in the toilet.

Nico runs to me and holds my hair back with one hand while using the other to rub my back in a comforting motion. "Dr. Watson said you would have morning sickness, which is normal and should go away in the next trimester."

I push myself up from the toilet. "I just need to take a shower and clean up."

"Okay, I'll make you some breakfast in the meantime."

The mention of breakfast makes my stomach roll. I feel like I won't ever be able to eat again.

Nico leans down kisses me, but I pull back thinking I just puked and probably smell. Instead, Nico just smiles down at me before leaving the bathroom to head downstairs and make breakfast.

He wasn't affected or grossed out by me at all.

His words once again playing in my head.

The way he looks at me. The way he touches me. The way he takes care of me.

He does love me.

But that doesn't change anything. He is still the enemy. Not mine but my family's. They would never forgive me if they found out.

Chapter 30

LILY

I take a quick shower, change clothes, and brush my teeth twice before heading downstairs.

I can smell bacon before I'm halfway down the hall. Unlike how I expected, I don't get the need to run to the bathroom and vomit.

I follow the smell to the kitchen and find Nico cooking bacon in a pan on the stove. He is wearing nothing but his boxers, and I can feel the warmth growing between my legs.

Not sure what I want more right now. Food or Nico.

Nico turns and places the bacon in a plate before looking up towards me. "I made bacon, toast and eggs. I wasn't sure what you were in the mood for."

I grab a plate from the counter. "Everything," I say as I make my way to the delicious and mouth-watering food. I don't think I've ever craved food this badly in my life.

Carter enters the kitchen while rubbing his eyes. "I see you made breakfast."

I'm about to fill up my plate when Nico covers my eyes with his hand. "Carter, have you ever fucking heard of clothes?"

"You're one to talk considering you're not wearing anything but boxers either."

I didn't even realise Carter wasn't wearing anything but boxers. The food has seemed to have gained all my attention.

Nico growls. "Well, I don't want Lily to be forced to see your half naked ass so go put on some clothes."

"Why? Afraid of a little competition?" Carter chuckles.

Nico makes a weird sound in his throat before swearing under his breathe, "Fucker."

I nudge Nico in the side. "Can I eat now?"

"Only with your eyes closed."

I frown. "How am I supposed to eat with my eyes closed?" This is just ridiculous.

I can't see it but for some reason I can sense Nico smiling. "I can always feed you."

I elbow Nico with all my force causing him to cough and drop his hand. "No thanks. I can feed myself thank you very much."

I start filling up my plate and walk over to the table Carter is currently sitting at with his mug of coffee. I take the seat beside him and I'm about to take a bite when Nico takes the seat on the other side of me and pulls my chair closer to him.

Carter looks up from his mug. "And here I thought Alessio had possessive issues."

"Shut up before I make you," Nico shoots back at Carter.

I tune out their bickering as I eat my food. Each bite feels like heaven in my mouth.

Nico and Carter are still taking shots at each other when I go back for seconds. By the time I have returned to the table, they have decided to a boxing match at the gym. Both threatening to knock the other out.

They sound like two kids squabbling over something silly. I'm not even entirely sure what they are arguing about.

Someone clears their throat behind me causing the room to go silent. I turn and look behind me to see a tall, brown haired and eyes man standing at the kitchen entrance. He is handsome at first glance but also deathly scary.

"Can I ask what the fuck you two are fighting about?" asks the mystery man.

Nico rises to his feet causing the chair to scratch against the floor as it is being pushed back. "Alessio, your *brother* is trying to piss me off."

Recognizing the name, I realise this must be Nico's older brother, the ruthless Capo of the Vitale family.

Carter laughs. "I did nothing but wake up. Alessio, your *crazy* brother has some issues."

"I have issues?" Nico points towards himself. "You're the one who refuses to wear pants and a shirt."

"See what I mean?"

Alessio sighs. "Emma and Daniele get along better then you two. I need to talk to the both of you in private."

Understanding, I get up from my seat. "I'll go back upstairs."

Nico turns to me. "No, you stay here. We will go into another room."

Carter rises to his feet and drops his mug in the sink before following Nico and Alessio out of the kitchen.

I get this nagging feeling that Alessio must have wanted to talk about something to do with me.

I go back to eating but this time, it tastes different.

I discard the last remaining bits of my food in the disposal and rinse my plate. I also wash the pan and dishes in the sink, needing to do something to keep busy.

NICO

I follow Alessio and Carter into Carter's penthouse office. Despite being an office, it's rarely ever used. Most of the time we work out of Encore or Alessio's office upstairs.

Carter shuts the office door behind us. "What's going on?"

Alessio showing up suddenly is not good news.

"I got a call this morning from the Mancini family," Alessio starts. I'm already hating where this is going. "They've captured Gia and want to make a trade, Gia for Lily."

"How the fuck did they get Gia?" I wonder out loud.

Alessio leans against the office desk. "Apparently she had gone to father's place last night. Her father sent the guard away saying he could protect his own daughter."

"Clearly he fucking can't," I point out the obvious. Gia's dad and brother are both useless. They can't do anything right. Which is why they are so low within the organization. The small amount of relevancy they have is due to Gia's marriage to me. Her family has tried to slither their way into a higher position for years.

"They gave us till tonight to make the arrangements, or they will send Gia back in pieces."

"I'm not giving them Lily."

"Nico," Alessio begins. "If we don't trade Gia for Lily, rumors will spread. How we let the Mancinis take one our women and we did nothing. I know you don't have feelings for Gia and hate her for all the shit she pulled but we can't just sit by and do nothing."

I hate that Alessio is right. This will be a huge hit to the organization, not to mention even those loyal to us will question how we let this happen. One of our cousins or other underbosses in other states might try and make a move to gain control seeing it as a moment of weakness. It would put my family in danger, including my niece and nephew.

As much as people fear us, they also respect us.

The thought of giving Lily back pierces through my heart.

Not only did Gia fucking make my life hell from day one but now she took away my one happiness and joy.

That is what Lily is in my life.

I want to tell Alessio no, I can't give up Lily and my unborn baby. But both my brothers have sacrificed and risked so much already for me.

Carter places a hand on my shoulder. "We will get Lily back another way."

I want to believe that, but I know once Lily is back home in Chicago, we won't be able to get near her. But I will die trying if I have too.

Chapter 31

LILY

After washing the dishes in the sink, I ran back upstairs for round two in the toilet bowl.

After cleaning myself up, I settled into bed to rest.

How could something so good make me feel so awful? Just thinking about what I ate makes me want to vomit.

After a while, the bedroom door squeaks open and Nico walks in and gets into bed beside me. Something doesn't feel right. I can't explain it, but I can sense something is off.

Nico wraps his arm around my shoulder and pulls me into him. "You get to finally go home."

I pull away from Nico. "What? You're letting me go?"

Nico smirks. "No, sweetheart, I'm never letting you go."

I am confused about what he is saying. "What do you mean I get to go home?"

"You get to go home for *now*." Before I can ask any questions, Nico continues, "Your family kidnapped Gia and want to make a trade. You for her." My family kidnapped Gia. "As much as I hate to return you to your family, I don't have a choice."

My heart feels like it's in my throat. "When?"

"Tonight."

I finally get to go home to my family. Back to Ronan. My heart drops to the pit of my stomach thinking about getting married to Ronan again.

Nico lifts my chin up with his hand and kisses me. I melt at his touch and the ache in my heart grows bigger.

Before I was able to hide my pain with anger. Anger of being used. Anger at getting played. But now that I know Nico loves me like I do him, the pain feels too raw. I can't mask the pain anymore.

A tear falls down my cheek and Nico pulls away while wiping my tear away with his thumb.

"I got you something." Nico pulls out a small black velvet box from his jacket pocket.

He hands it to me, and I open it. It's an emerald necklace.

"It reminded me of your eyes." He pulls out the necklace and pushes my hair to the side. He places it around my neck and locks it in place.

I can't get any words out. Too many emotions are stuck in my throat.

He gives me a small smile. "Don't get too comfortable once your home. I will come back for you and our baby."

I know he will.

Chapter 32

LILY

We pull up at an abandon parking lot around midnight. There is not a single car or person in the distance.

Nico and I are sitting in the back with Carter and Alessio in the front.

I go to open the door and Nico grabs my hand. "Not yet. You stay in the SUV until I say so."

A black SUV with tinted windows pulls up across from us.

Alessio and Carter step out with their guns drawn in their hands.

From the SUV across from us, Enzo and my cousin Antonio step out.

Alessio and Carter raise their guns towards them as do my brother and cousin at Nico's brothers.

A string tugs at my heart at my family getting injured.

I don't want my brother and cousin to get hurt because of me. They think they are coming here to save me from monsters but in reality I'm perfectly fine. I don't even have a scratch on me.

"Where is Gia?" Alessio calls out.

"Show us Lily first," Enzo responds.

Nico gets out of the SUV, grabs my arm, and pulls me out with him.

The wind hits my face and I get a shiver down my spine when my eyes lock with Enzo. I can see the relief on his face from seeing me.

If only he knew the truth, then he would hate me.

Enzo nods to someone inside the SUV behind him and Enzo's best friend and my family's enforcer, Marco, steps out. He drags someone out with him and I see that it is Gia. Her mouth is completely taped shut and her hands are tied together.

Gia wiggles in Marco's grasp and he drags her towards Enzo and Antonio and drops her face first on to the ground with a loud thud in front of their feet. Marco smirks when Gia hits the ground. Gia squirms and is trying to say something but with the tape covering her mouth makes it hard to understand.

"Send my sister over," Enzo says.

"No," Alessio responds, "We trade at the same time. And don't fucking try anything unless you want Lily to get hurt."

Nico's grip on my arms tightens for a millisecond before loosening it.

Nico takes a step forward with me and Enzo motions for Marco to go. Marco frowns down at Gia before pulling her up by the arm and moves forward towards us.

Gia struggles in Marco's hold which causes her to lose her step. Not waiting for her to get her feet planted on the ground, Marco drags Gia along like a sack of potatoes.

In the middle of the empty parking lot once I am a few inches away from Marco, he lets Gia drop to the ground once again. "Hand me Lily and take your trash." Marco motions for me to come towards him.

I go to take a step towards Marco, but Nico doesn't let me go. I peer up at Nico and I can't read his face.

VENGEFUL PRINCE

Sensing the tension in the night air from both ends, I pull my arm away gently from Nico's grasp. He looks down at me and for a second I see hurt in his eyes before it's gone.

I want to tell Nico how much I love him and that I don't blame him for anything. I know he blames himself but I'm the one who betrayed her family. If I did what I was told, this wouldn't have happened. But I can't. Not right here, not now with everyone watching.

I swallow down the lump forming in my throat at the thought of saying goodbye and walk towards Marco.

Marco quickly grabs me and pulls me towards my brother and cousin. I'm being pushed into the SUV and I can't help but look back one last time.

Nico is still standing at the same spot as Enzo and Antonio walk backwards to the SUV with their guns still drawn.

My eyes lock with Nico before I'm pushed inside the SUV.

This is goodbye.

Chapter 33

LILY

Antonio zipped it out of the parking lot and is speeding down the street when Enzo sitting in the passenger seat turns around and looks at me. "Lily, are you okay? They didn't hurt you, did they?"

My throat feels clogged, and I try to force out words. "I…I…" Tears cascade down my face like a waterfall. "I'm…. Enzo." My voice cracks at the mention of my brother's name.

My brother grasps my hand into his. "It's going to be okay. We will make them pay for this."

I want to tell my brother: I'm fine. They didn't hurt me. Don't hurt them. But each time I try and open my mouth, the pain is too strong.

I wipe my tears with the back of my hand. "I'm sorry." I'm sorry for betraying you and the family. I'm sorry for putting you at risk by having you try and save me for no reason.

"Stop Lily, it's not your fault," Enzo soothes.

"If anyone is at fault, it's those fucking Vitales," Marco adds. I get the urge to defend Nico but stop myself.

A car with bright headlights passes us by and I notice a red scratch on the side of Marco's face.

"You're injured." I point towards the scratch. My voice comes out better now that we aren't talking about me or the Vitales.

Antonio laughs from the driver seat. "I wouldn't consider that an injury."

"What happened?" I ask.

Marco rubs the area where the scratch is. "Nico Vitale's bitch wife scratched me with her long ass nails. I should have cut her face up for the shit she pulled."

I wince at the thought of Marco cutting up Gia's face. She wasn't the nicest person to me but considering I was sleeping with her husband, I can't blame her.

Gia also was kidnapped by my family, and I doubt they treated her the same way I was by the Vitales.

"You didn't hurt her, did you?" I probe.

"No, didn't get the chance since your brother wouldn't let me touch her."

"We needed her to get Lily back," Enzo admits. "We couldn't risk killing her, even though she was the most annoying person I have ever met. I don't know how the fuck Vitale hasn't strangled the bitch yet."

"She might have just been scared since she was kidnapped." I don't know why I'm trying to make excuses for Gia. Maybe out of guilt.

Marco huffs, "No, that bitch is straight up crazy. Something isn't right with her up here." Marco taps the side of his temple. Coming from Marco that says something. Marco isn't the family enforcer for no reason. Some people say he has issues, but he's always been known as my brother's friend to me.

Enzo's phone rings and he picks it up. "Yeah, we got her. We will be home soon." Enzo hangs up the call and looks back at me. "It's Papa. He's waiting for us to return."

My heart pounds in my chest at having to face Papa and Mama.

I look down at my hands on my lap, letting my hair fall forward and cover the shame I feel is on my face.

"Don't worry Lily, you're safe now. You will be home soon," Enzo remarks.

NICO

Carter helped Gia get up after the Mancini family dropped her face first into the ground.

I could have helped her, but I was preoccupied watching the woman I love leave.

During the exchange, I had second thoughts and wanted to drag Lily back with me.

But then she pulled away from me and walked towards her brother, her family.

She did what she thought was the best thing considering the night would have ended with a shoot out if I tried to take Lily back. Yet the twinge at her going was agonizing.

I walk back to the SUV and hear Gia screech behind me before opening the opposite side of the SUV door and settling in.

Carter gets into the driver seat and Alessio in the passenger seat as the SUV is started up. Carter puts it into motion, and we head back towards the city.

"You better make them pay for this!" Gia screams. "They broke my fucking nose! Those barbarians treated me like trash. I want their heads!"

"Shut the fuck up!" I scream into Gia's face.

She flinches back at my sudden reaction and then snarls, "You're telling me to shut up. You're to blame for this. It was your whore's family that kidnapped me! I want revenge for what they did!"

Alessio turns around. "You're not fucking getting nothing. You don't call the orders around here. Don't fucking forget that. As for your nose, it was fucked up before you were kidnapped."

Gia clenches her fist together in anger but doesn't respond. She knows better than to piss off Alessio.

We drive back in silence aside from the occasional murmuring by Gia under her breath.

Meanwhile, my thoughts are filled with how I'm going to get Lily back.

Chapter 34

LILY

After 10 hours of driving, we finally arrive in Chicago. My home. Or what was home before. It doesn't feel the same. I feel like I'm missing something. *Nico.*

We go through our house gates and drive up the long driveway and stop in front of the house. My home once.

I step out and head towards the front door when it flies open and my mama comes running out while crying. She instantly runs into me and pulls me into a hug so tight I get smothered in the crook of her neck. She quickly pulls away and looks me up and down with red eyes filled with tears.

Looking at her closely, she has dark bags under her eyes and her hair is a mess. This is the first time I've ever seen her like this. Even when Enzo was stabbed, she didn't react like this.

My mama keeps touching me gently with shaky hands as if she doesn't believe I'm here.

Seeing her like this causes me to well up in pain.

"My daughter," she cries as she pulls me into another hug.

I hug her back and cry for the pain she has suffered because of me.

"Claudia, let the girl go," I hear my papa say from behind my mama.

But she doesn't let me go but continues to cry and I can't get myself to let go either. All this time I've thought she didn't care about me. She has undergone so much ache because of me. I don't deserve her tears or hug.

Papa pulls Mama away from me with force. With her eyes still red and cheeks blotched with tears, she gives me a smile. "You're home and safe now."

"Come inside, Lily." My papa motions towards the house. Unlike Mama, he looks well put together, but I can see some dark circles under his eyes, like Mama's.

Enzo puts an arm around my shoulders and tugs me towards the house.

Once settled in the living room, I know what's coming.

"Claudia, why don't you prepare something for Lily to eat?" Papa orders.

My mama gets up from the couch. "Of course. My daughter must be starving. I'll see what we have in the kitchen, I'm sure the cook has something in fridge for me to heat up." She walks out of the room, and I feel the air in the room shift.

Papa takes a seat across from me, while Enzo stands to the side.

"Lily, I need you to tell me everything. Start from the beginning. How you got kidnapped and what they did. Don't miss one detail," Papa commands.

My throat goes dry with Papa's gaze settled on me. "When I was getting ready, someone came in," I get down to explaining. "I thought it was Enzo first to come get me for the ceremony. But it was Nico."

"Nico Vitale." Papa is not asking but making note.

I nod. "He stabbed me a needle that knocked me out. They kept me at a penthouse somewhere in New York." I don't mention it's Carter's.

"You called Enzo, how did you end up doing that? It was early morning from what I recall," Papa interrogates.

"When Nico was asleep, I took his phone and called." I cringe at using the word asleep. How do I explain why Nico was asleep in the same room as me?

Papa's jaw twitches. "Enzo said he heard a loud noise and scream before the call was disconnected."

"I got caught." I look down at the floor, "I'm sorry, Papa." My voice is quiet and I begin to shake. I know I need to confess everything, but I can't look up, let alone speak.

Papa pushes up from his seat and walks over to me. His hand comes out and I flinch expecting him to hit me.

After a few seconds, I look up when I don't feel anything.

I peer at my papa's face and for once he looks at me with sadness. He gently pats my head. "You've been through a lot. Why don't you go upstairs and rest? I'll have your mama send up the food."

I slowly rise from the couch and look towards my brother and he too has the same look my papa does.

I walk out of the living room and head upstairs.

If I thought I couldn't feel any more guilt, I was wrong.

Chapter 35

3 MONTHS LATER

LILY

It's been three months since I was kidnapped. Despite thinking I would continue with my wedding to Ronan, it never happened.

Ronan had refused to help my family when I was taken. I wasn't worth sacrificing his men to infiltrate Vitale territory to find me. Papa took offense to this and cancelled his alliance with him.

My papa nor Enzo haven't asked any more questions about my kidnapping since I arrived.

Occasionally I will see them stare at me with sadness but quickly hide it. As much as I want to tell them they have nothing to feel sad about, I can't. The moment that I do, they will look at me with hate.

My bump hasn't grown to be noticeable, and I have worn baggy clothes to try and hide it as much as possible.

I ordered prenatal vitamins online and have been taking them secretly. Eventually I won't be able to hide it anymore from my family.

I read a couple articles online about girls hiding their entire pregnancy and giving birth in their rooms by themselves. I don't know how they could do it. But I know their families aren't like mine. In the mafia, you need to be aware of every detail around you.

Enzo had pointed out a few days ago I have been eating more than usual. I tried to eat less and when I did crave food, I would hold out until the kitchen was empty and sneak in to eat without anyone's knowledge.

It's Thanksgiving and the house is full of staff. My parents are throwing their annual Thanksgiving dinner.

I make my way to the kitchen, passing by Mama. She smiles at me as I walk by. She's been doing a lot of that lately. Paying attention to me.

Before I could walk up to her and be in the same room as her and half the time, she wouldn't even notice my presence.

When I get to the kitchen the scent of food being cooked churns my stomach. Despite being 4 months in, the morning sickness hasn't stopped.

I read online it could last throughout your pregnancy and some recommended seeing a doctor. I don't have the option of going to a doctor as it would raise too many questions.

I take a step inside the kitchen and the smell and sight of food is too much. I feel the contents of my stomach ready to come out.

I spin on my heels and run to the downstairs bathroom and puke into the toilet bowl.

I'm heaving into the bowl when I hear my mama's voice. "Lily, what's wrong? Are you sick? I'm going to call a doctor right now." She turns to call a doctor when I quickly push to my feet.

"No, Mama. I'm fine I don't need to see a doctor."

"You're not fine. You might have caught something. The doctor needs to examine you."

Knowing what the doctor will say after examining me, I try and stop my mama.

"No, please don't call the doctor," I plead.

Mama's eyebrows snap together. "What's going on, Lily? Either you tell me, or I call the doctor."

I look down at the floor, not being able to face my mama. "I'm pregnant." I finally tell the truth.

Mama takes a step back in shock hitting her hip on the bathroom counter. "Y-you're pregnant? How can this be? Ronan wasn't supposed to touch you before the wedding."

"It's not Ronan's."

Mama comes closer. "One of the Vitale's'?" she asks in a hushed voice.

I nod feeling the shame rise and flow through my body. "It's Nico Vitale's," I finally come clean.

Mama gasps and covers her mouth with her hand. "I'll talk to your papa and brother. You go upstairs and stay in your room. Don't come out."

I head to my room and take a seat on my bed, waiting for my execution for my betrayal.

Chapter 36

LILY

I hear glass shattering downstairs. One after another.

A number of the staff members at the house have run out of the house and are waiting in the driveway at the sudden commotion.

I hear a knock on the door and I'm expecting Papa to come in with his gun to finish me off.

I'm surprised when the door opens and Enzo pops his head in.

"Can I come in?" Enzo asks.

I nod and take a seat on the bed.

Enzo walks into my room and takes a seat next to me. I can't look him in the eyes or face him. Instead, I look to the ground and divert my gaze.

"Mama told Papa the Nico Vitale raped you."

My head snaps up at Enzo in horror. "She said what?"

"You're not going to deny it," Enzo says, more as a statement then a question.

Of course, I am going to deny it because that's not happened.

"Listen to me, Lily. I know what happened, but if you deny it, you will bring shame to yourself and our family. This is your out."

I shake my head. "No, Enzo you don't know what happened." I try and think where to start. How to explain what happened between me and Nico.

Enzo interrupts my thoughts. "I do know, Lily. Nico Vitale's wife has a big mouth."

"You know?"

"I do. But that doesn't change anything. The Vitales knew who you were and they targeted you. They tricked you and when that wasn't enough they kidnapped you." Enzo's face is filled with hate and anger.

"It wasn't like that. It's true Nico knew who I was and did get close to me to get to Ronan but—"

"There's no fucking but, Lily!" Enzo stands and paces the room. "You will tell Papa and everyone that Nico Vitale forced himself on you. Unless you want Papa to kill you and your baby."

"Papa wouldn't." My voice barely above a whisper. I accepted my death for my betrayal, but my baby did nothing.

"He wouldn't have a choice. If it gets out that you betrayed the family—" Enzo stops talking as his throat muscles tightens at whatever he was going to say.

"Does anyone else know about me and Nico?"

"Antonio and Marco but they promised me they would keep quiet." Enzo comes and crouches down in front of me. "Please Lily, promise me you will tell Papa that you were forced and in return I will protect you and your child any way I can."

For the first time, I see terror in my brother's eyes. Terror for me if the truth comes out.

I place my hand on top of Enzo's. "I promise."

Enzo nods and rises to his full height. "Okay, Papa wants to see you downstairs."

I stand but feel a weight around my shoulders dragging me down.

I follow Enzo downstairs to my papa's office, and as I walk past the living room, I see everything is shattered or flipped over.

As we get closer to papa's office, my heart beats faster with each step. By the time we arrive in front of his door, the throbbing in my ear from heart is so loud, I don't even hear Enzo.

He places his hands on my shoulders. "Don't forget your promise, Lily." I nod since I can't seem to open my mouth. Enzo turns the doorknob and walks into Papa's office. I follow close behind him to the point that when he stops, I almost hit his back due to the lack of distance.

I hear a high cry from the side and look over to see my mama sitting on the couch crying her eyes out.

Papa is sitting at his desk and doesn't look up at me.

"It's been more then three months since the kidnapping so I'm to assume it's too late for an abortion?" Papa asks.

I didn't even consider abortion an option. Even when the doctor in the emergency room offered it to me or when I first found out about who Nico was. It was never an option to me because I couldn't hurt my baby.

I look at Papa, and when his gaze snaps at me, I can't help but look down again.

"I'm sorry, Papa," I apologize quietly.

"You will stay inside for the next few months. Once the baby is born, we will deal with it then. But for now, it stays within these walls. No one will know about this," Papa strains.

I nod quickly wanting to leave.

Papa waves his head for me to leave, and I run out of his office the first chance I get.

Chapter 37

FIVE MONTHS LATER

LILY

The sky is full of dark clouds and rain. April used to be my least favorite month due to all the showers that stream down from the sky all month long. But now with my baby being due any day, I'm starting to love this month.

My parents still think I have a month left and haven't questioned the enormous size the bump is.

Enzo had a doctor come in to check on me and the baby every few weeks. My baby boy is growing so quickly inside me.

Enzo made sure to have the doctor provide the incorrect due date to Papa just in case.

It's early morning and the sky is dark from the clouds.

I push myself up from my bed and walk barefoot to the kitchen. Papa fired the home staff a few months ago when my bump was starting to get noticeable.

There had been rumors flying already about what the Vitales did to me while I was kidnapped.

I had heard Marco and Enzo talking about how people thought I was mentally unstable due to the torture inflicted on me.

Papa had said after I have the baby, I needed to make a grand appearance to show everyone I am okay, and he will soon arrange another marriage for me.

The thought of marrying someone is painful to even think about. As the daughter of a Capo, I shouldn't be surprised. But I doubt I will have many offers considering I'm tainted in the eyes of the mafia and have a baby as baggage.

I'm walking past Papa's office when I hear Enzo talking. "She thinks she's going to raise the baby. You need to tell her the truth."

"She doesn't need to know," Papa responds.

They're talking about me and my baby. Why wouldn't I raise my child? I press myself closer to the door.

"Papa, I know you think this is best for Lily, but she will never forgive you when she finds out your plan of giving her child away," Enzo claims.

I'm frozen in the spot. They were going to give my child away. The room starts to spin, and I feel myself being swallowed by the floor.

"Enough Enzo," Papa barks. "It is not Lily's child, it's that fucking bastard's child! I will not have my daughter ruined. Everyone already knows she has been dishonored, and with a child, *his child*, she will never be accepted."

My eyes fill up with tears and they stream down my face. I whirl on my heels and run back to my room.

They were going to take my child away from me and give him away.

I lay in bed remembering the conversation about my marriage after having the baby and I realize not once was it mentioned the baby would come with me.

The baby kicks inside me; I place my hand over my bump and decide then I need to leave.

If I stay, Papa will take my baby from me no matter what I say or do. I could kick, scream, and beg and he will still take my baby away.

I change out of my pajamas and into a shirt with leggings and boots. Once I have put on my jacket, I realize I have no real means of escape or money.

I can't exactly use my papa's credit card to go on the run. I would be found and dragged home within an hour.

I look out the window and see the gardener's truck parked outside. I grab my purse without thinking and tip toe downstairs.

Mama is still sleeping, considering it's still early, and Papa and Enzo are pre-occupied in Papa's office.

I use the side door and make sure none of the guards see me before I make my way to the gardener's pickup truck.

I climb into the back and hide in the corner behind a bunch of equipment and a lawnmower.

I ball myself up to try and make myself smaller and wait.

It feels like hours pass before I hear the back of the truck open. My heart thumps against my chest at the thought of getting caught. After a few minutes, the back is closed, and the front door opens and closes.

The truck beneath me vibrates when it starts and I feel it move into motion.

Each second my heart thumps louder at the thought of the guards catching me or Papa finding out I have escaped and discovering me.

The truck stops and I hear chatter. The baby kicks me hard, and I suck in my breath to stay quiet.

The truck again is put into motion and continues for a few more minutes. After a while I hear a car honk and cars passing by. Realizing I have made it out of my home, I peak out of my spot.

I wait for the truck to stop at a red-light and push out of my spot and quickly jump out. I look back and see the gardener has the music blaring and doesn't even notice me.

I run to the sidewalk and the light turns green and the truck drives away.

I run and stand underneath shelter from the rain in front of a tattoo shop. I pull out my wallet and calculate how much cash I have. I have a few hundred dollars which won't be enough to live off for more than a few days, let alone raise a baby.

I regret not taking some of my jewelry to pawn off. My hand rubs the emerald diamond around my neck. I could pawn the gift Nico gave me. The thought of parting with it is excruciating.

Or I could go back to New York, *to Nico*.

He would protect me and our child. I know it in my heart. It's the best option.

I walk a few blocks in the rain trying to get to the train station but my feet ache from being pregnant. I find a taxi to take me the rest of the way to the station and buy a ticket to New York City.

Chapter 38

LILY

After a few hours on the train, I finally arrive to New York City. It would have been faster to fly but I couldn't risk using my passport.

It's Friday night and I take a taxi to Encore.

I don't know where Nico lives exactly but I remember my brother and his friends talking about the club the Vitales owned and how popular it was.

The taxi driver pulls up in front of Encore and I see a long line of people going around the block.

I pay the driver and step out. I walk over to the front of the line and I can see girls staring me up and down. Probably at the pregnant girl trying to get into a club while looking like a mess from the rain.

Thankfully it's not raining here, and my hair and jacket has dried but it's a mess compared to the girls dressed in short dresses and heels standing in line.

I get to the front of the line and a huge bouncer in a black t-shirt turns around and faces me. He looks me up and down, like those in the line and smirks. "Lost, little girl?"

"No, I'm here to see Nico Vitale," I say while keeping my voice even and steady.

"Go home little girl, this place isn't for you." The large man crosses his arm and blocks me from entering.

"Not before seeing Nico." I need to see him. I have nowhere else to go.

"He isn't here so you're wasting your time."

"Then Alessio Vitale or Carter Vitale."

The large bouncer stares down at me with a glare. "Don't waste my time. I would hate to have to throw a pregnant girl to the curb."

I swallow down the image of me being chucked like a ball to the street and don't falter from why I came here.

"Tell Alessio that Lily…" I almost say my last name but stop remembering I am the enemy. "Tell him Lily is here to see him. He will know who I am and if he doesn't want to see me, then by all means throw me to the curb."

The bouncer glares at me for a beat to long before speaking, "Fine, wait here. But if the boss cuts out my tongue for wasting his time, I plan to take my anger out on you."

I shudder at the thought. Alessio wouldn't cut out a man's tongue for something as little as this. Of course, Alessio didn't get his title for being ruthless for no reason.

As I'm waiting, I pull my jacket around me tighter to keep out the cold. I couldn't zip it up since my bump gets in the way.

The bouncer returns and he doesn't seem to be bleeding out of his mouth, so I take it as a good sign.

He raises the red velvet rope. "Follow me."

I walk past the bouncer and don't miss the glares I get from women standing in line.

I follow him inside into a dark hallway. As we get further down, the music gets louder with each step. At the end of the hallway, we enter a large room with music blaring so loud that the entire room shakes from the noise. Men and women are dancing up against each other. Some are a sweaty mess, others a drunk mess. There are also two bars with people standing around drinking and getting completely wasted.

We walk past a number of people who stagger by with big smiles on their faces as they enjoy their night.

At the end of the room, there is another hallway that we take until we reach stairs. I groan at having to climb them as my legs feel like they are going to give out at any second.

The stupid bouncer doesn't slow down as I climb the stairs but instead scowls at me from the top of the stairs at having to wait for me.

Once I take the last step, we go past a large room filled with monitors of the entire club security feed until we stop in front of a door.

The bouncer knocks on the door lightly and then opens it slowly. He doesn't go in but instead nudges me in. Once inside, the door behind me closes shut.

For a large man he sure is a scaredy cat.

I look around the room and see a bar on one end and a large desk with wall to ceiling windows above the club behind it. I walk over to the window and see the entire club from up here.

I hear the door open behind me and close and I turn around at the noise.

Alessio stands in front of the door with his hands in his pockets. Blocking my only exit.

Now I'm starting to wish I had asked for Carter instead. I don't know Alessio well and we haven't even spoken a word to each other.

Alessio looks me up and down before making his way to me. "When Johnny told me you were here, I was sure he was lying. That or another Lily was trying to see me." He stops in front of me and assesses me.

I don't know what he is trying to find. "I didn't have anywhere to go."

"You were back home with your family."

Alessio's powerful gaze makes me take a step back. "My family wanted to take my baby from me, so I left. I don't have anywhere to go." I sigh, realizing this may have been a bad idea. "I can leave if you don't want to help me." I don't know where I will go but I will figure it out as long as I have my baby with me.

I walk past Alessio and head towards the door when Alessio stops me. "I will help you. After all you are carrying my brother's child."

"Illegitimate child," I correct Alessio. My son will never be accepted into the mafia, not in our world. The thought that my son will be painted as something less squeezes at my heart.

"Still his blood, our blood. Nico and Carter are out of state for business. I will let Nico know you're here. In the meantime, you can stay in one of my guestrooms until Nico comes back. It's the safest option."

As much as I don't want to stay at Alessio's, I don't really have a choice. I'm down to less than a hundred dollars and that won't even buy you a cheap hotel in this city for a night.

Also, if Nico is out of town with Carter, I can't stay at Carter's penthouse I stayed in previously. It wouldn't be right with him not being around. Nico's place is out of the question since I'm sure Gia is living there.

I'll just have to stay with Alessio until Nico comes back. Hopefully he comes back soon.

Chapter 39

LILY

Once we get to the penthouse, Alessio showed me to the guest room. Noticing I didn't bring any clothes with me, he brought me some of his wife's sleepwear and clothes to borrow. I'm thankful to him despite him scaring me slightly.

I use the bathroom to shower and clean myself before changing and getting into bed.

I fall asleep as soon as I hit the mattress from the long journey and the exhaustion of running around all day.

I'm woken up to a small poke to my cheek. I open my eyes and see a little girl that resembles a doll with brown hair and brown eyes hovering over me.

"Who are you?" the little girl asks.

I rub my eyes to be fully awake. "Lily." I look around and see it's daylight now.

The little girl smiles widely. "Hi Lily, I'm Emma."

I smile back at the little girl. "It's nice to meet you, Emma."

Emma gently touches my stomach. "Is there a girl in there? I already have a brother and want a sister to play with."

I smile at the little girl but before I can respond the bedroom door opens and a beautiful blonde with striking ice blue eyes walks in. "Emma! I told you not to bother our guest."

Emma pouts and crosses her arms. "But Mommy, she might have a sister for me to play with."

She picks Emma up. "That's not how it works, Emma. Not everyone that is pregnant is going to have a sister for you." The blonde turns to me. "I'm so sorry. I told her not to wake you, but she slipped past me while I was feeding my son Daniele."

I push to a sitting position. "It's okay. Your daughter is lovely."

She smiles instantly at my compliment. "She is, isn't she?" she says before giving Emma a kiss on the cheek. "I'm Alessio's wife Anna. Breakfast is ready if you're hungry."

"I'll be out in a minute after I wash up."

Anna smiles before turning to walk out with Emma in her arms who is no longer pouting.

I get out of bed and head to the bathroom. After washing my face and brushing my teeth, I make my way out to the kitchen.

Anna is sitting at the table feeding a baby boy on one side with Emma on her other side. She takes turns between the two children to make sure they are fed while her food sits cold in front of her. From the smile on her face, I don't think she minds.

When I step further into the kitchen, she notices my presence and looks up at me with a smile. "Lily, come sit. I'll grab a plate with some food for you."

I stick out my arms to stop her. "No, it's okay. I can grab my own food. You already have your hands full with two kids."

She waves a hand in the air. "I don't mind. Sit, you're a guest in our house."

Emma turns in her seat. "Come sit with me!" Her voice is filled with cheer and excitement.

I walk over to the table and take a seat next to Emma who beams at me. Anna walks over and places a plate full of food in front of me before taking her seat in between her two children.

Since leaving yesterday morning, I've barely eaten. I could eat a horse right now and I wouldn't complain.

"Alessio had to go work but he told me Nico will be home by this afternoon. I'm sure he will be glad to see you."

"He will?" I ask. I can't help but wonder what Anna knows about me. Does she know who my family is and how I'm technically the enemy and a mistress?

Anna smiles brightly. "Of course he will. I know he has been trying for months to get to you in Chicago, but your family has blocked all paths in and put reinforcements in to make sure anyone who looks like Nico, or his family, didn't cross the border."

"He tried to go to Chicago?" This entire time I thought he moved on and forgot about me, us. I place my hand on my bump and feel my boy kick inside.

"Why wouldn't he? He loves you and I know he has always wanted children but G—" Anna stops and I see panic in her face at almost mentioning Gia. "Sorry I didn't mean to bring up, you know who."

I give her a reassuring smile. "It's okay." I am the other woman, I should be the one who's embarrassed.

We eat silently after that, but it doesn't last long since Emma starts to tell me about her ballet classes and how she wants to become a ballerina when she grows up.

She is the most precious thing I have ever seen and consider having a girl one day. Then the realisation of my situation crashes on me and pushes away all thoughts of having a girl.

NICO

The pilot said we would be landing in two hours but that's too long for me. I had asked, or more like demanded, the pilot go faster but he claimed he was going as fast he could for us to make it back to the city alive.

I slump into the cream leather chair across from Carter. "We need a new fucking pilot. This one is too fucking slow."

"He is a good pilot. I did a thorough screening and testing before I hired him. Don't fucking make him quit because it's a hassle for me to find a new pilot."

"I need to get to the city sooner."

"Lily isn't going anywhere. Relax, we will be home soon." Carter opens his laptop and starts to type. I on the other hand can't do any work right now. My mind keeps drifting to Lily.

When Alessio called last night and informed me Lily was back in New York City looking for me, I was sure I had hallucinated him saying that. Lily couldn't be back in my territory and looking for me of all people.

She was back home in Chicago, where she belonged, yet she left and came back. I wanted to think she came back for me, but I know better. She came back for our baby.

Alessio had also filled me in on the Mancini family trying to give our baby away. I clench and unclench my fists in anger at the thought of my baby being thrown away by the Mancinis.

Carter looks up from his laptop. "Don't fuck this up this time."

"What?" My mind is still filled with rage.

"Don't fuck this up with Lily. She came willingly. She abandoned her family and gave up everything to come back. I'm sure it wasn't easy. So don't fuck this up. Don't give her a reason to regret coming back."

I look at my younger brother and I see so much emotion in his face. I know he is thinking about his past and how he lost his love. The darkness is slowly consuming him at just the memory. It does that with Carter. The memory of the past and what he lost.

"I won't. I will never give Lily a reason to regret coming back to me. I will give her everything within my power, give her everything she deserves." I want to give her my name and claim her as mine. But I can't. Not with Gia as my wife.

Lily deserves so much more than I can offer her. She deserves to be respected, not have to be called names or shamed.

Carter slowly comes out of the darkness he momentarily went to. "Good because I like Lily."

I narrow my eyes at Carter. "Like? What does that mean." I know my brother doesn't think of Lily like that, but I hate the idea of him even being fond of her for some reason. Maybe I do have possessive issues.

Carter chuckles. "Seriously you and Alessio need to get yourself checked out. I can call Dr. Watson when we land."

"Fuck off." I give Carter the middle finger just in case my words aren't enough.

But the little fucker only smiles wider.

The plane starts to descend and the thought of seeing Lily fills me with joy. This time I'm not letting her go, no matter what.

Chapter 40

LILY

I borrowed Anna's phone so I could call Enzo. I'm sure he is probably worried about me. I left without saying goodbye or leaving so much as a note to the one and only member of my family who has supported and loved me.

I saw an opportunity to run and took it. Had it been only about me, I would have risked finding Enzo and saying goodbye, but I had to think about my baby first.

I'm pacing in Alessio and Anna's guest room trying to forge the confidence to call.

The thought that Enzo will be disappointed or upset hurts. I didn't just betray the family, I betrayed him. After everything he did to get me back home and the lengths he went to keep me safe, I ran away.

I dial my brother's number and hover my thumb over the green call button. I force myself to hit the button and put the phone to my ear.

It rings a few times before I hear my brother speak on the other line.

"Hello?"

"Enzo, it's me, Lily."

There is silence for a few seconds that churns my stomach.

"I'm to assume by the New York number, you went back. Back to him?" The last word spoken with disgust.

I stupidly nod not being able to say the words out loud and realize he can't see me. I force the emotions rising up my throat down. "Yes."

"Why?"

"You are asking why?" My tone sounds accusatory. I push aside remembering Enzo was trying to protect me. "I heard you and Papa talking yesterday morning. I know he was going to take my baby away."

"I would have made sure the baby went to good parents."

"I will be a good parent," I snap. "My baby is mine and you were going to help Papa take him away from me."

"What else were we supposed to do? Let you raise that monster's child? No man within the organization would have agreed to marry you, even if you were the Capo's daughter. There are already dozens of rumors about you and a baby wouldn't help."

"I don't care! I don't care to get married to a man who I wouldn't have loved and who wouldn't have loved me back either. I would have been happy as long as I had my baby."

Enzo goes silent again for a few seconds before speaking. "You can't come back anymore. Word has spread that you ran away to the enemy and Papa plans on publicly disowning you for your actions. You will be considered a traitor."

His words feel like a knife slowly being pushed into my heart with each word he speaks. Disowned. Traitor.

"I know. I made my choice. I'm sorry, Enzo. I'm thankful for everything you have done but I have to put my baby first."

"I won't let you live with your head down. You don't deserve this. I will fix this. I promise. Good-bye, Lily." With that, he ends the call.

I collapse onto the bed. There is no fixing this. I will never be allowed to go back.

My baby boy kicks me hard, reminding me why I left my family. I drop the phone on the bed beside me and rub my bump with both my hands. "We are going to be okay," I whisper to my bump.

The bedroom door squeaks open and Nico walks in slowly. His gaze is set on me and he looks at me weirdly before masking it. "You came back."

I push to my feet and stand. "I didn't have anywhere to go. I know you are married and by me coming here I'm causing you problems…"

"You're not. I'm happy you came back." Nico clears his throat. "How is the baby?"

I smile down at my bump and gently rub it. "He's fine. He's been jumping around inside me all day."

"He?"

"Yes, he's a boy."

Nico slowly smiles. "I'm going to have a son." He walks over to me. "Do you mind if I feel him?"

I shake my head and grab Nico's hand to pull it towards my bump. Our boy kicks hard at the touch and Nico's eyes flicker with joy.

I'm over the moon that Nico is happy to have us but a nagging part of me keeps reminding myself I am the other woman, and my son will never be accepted.

NICO

I've moved Lily back downstairs into Carter's penthouse. I want her next to me at all times where I can keep an eye on her.

When I walked into Alessio's guest bedroom and saw her, I couldn't believe my eyes. She's even more beautiful than I remembered her.

Despite being 9 months pregnant, she still looks the same aside from the bump in the front.

She is currently resting upstairs in my bedroom. It took all my will power to leave her. I could have laid next to her bed and watched her sleep for hours.

I walk into Carter's living room where both my brothers are waiting for me.

"How bad is the damage?" I ask my brother Alessio.

"Not that bad for us anyways. Lorenzo Mancini has publicly disowned Lily and declared her a traitor. She will never be allowed back in Chicago anymore."

"Fuck them. She doesn't need them."

"They are her family," Carter reminds me. "I doubt she will be okay with her family cutting ties with her."

Fuck. As much as I'm happy Lily is here, I hate that she had to give up everything to be here.

"She can stay here for the time being, but she will have to be moved," Alessio says. "She can't be staying here with Gia one penthouse above. It wouldn't look good."

"I don't care how it looks," I seethe. I could care less what Gia thinks either.

"You should, considering it would affect Lily's reputation. The Mancinis have already spread rumors that we kidnapped and tortured Lily. Most think you forced yourself on her. At the moment most people pity her but if she stays here the rumors will work against her. She will be known as the other woman. We all know what kind of status they have in our world."

I recall being angry at Lily calling herself a whore but I might just go on a murderous killing spree if someone else calls her that. She doesn't deserve that title.

Alessio pats my shoulder. "I'll make arrangements to have Lily moved to a new penthouse nearby. It'll take a few weeks to put in bulletproof glass and get the security system put in place but in the meantime, it's best we only let those we trust know about Lily being here."

"Okay." I walk back up the stairs and go towards my bedroom. I slowly open the door and walk in. Lily is laying on her back asleep with one hand resting on her bump. She is giving me everything and all I ever did was take from her.

Chapter 41

LILY

Nico has been acting weird for the last couple of days since I came back. He gets excited one second and the next I see sadness in his eyes that he tries to hide from me.

He thinks I don't notice the turmoil playing within his head, but I do. Only because I have those same feelings inside mine.

I'm happy I'm with Nico again and our baby will be safe but at the same time I know the labels we will hold in our world.

I walk to the living room and find Nico sitting on the couch with his laptop. He has been working from the penthouse since he moved me back into Carter's place.

I take a seat across from him on the other couch. Needing the distance between us, otherwise I will get blinded by his warmth, smell and annoyingly handsome face and forget the conversation I came to have.

"Nico, we need to talk."

Nico raises his head up from his laptop. "About what?" He continues typing away on his laptop as he speaks.

"About us. About our baby."

Nico stops typing and closes his laptop. "What about us and our baby?"

"What will happen to us? I know how things work in our world. We will never have a place there. I will be known as the mistress and our son will be called a bastard."

Anger flashes across Nico's face. "Anyone who calls you or our son that will get a bullet in their head."

"Then you're going to have to kill your entire organization and every organization out there because that is what we will be known as."

The sadness Nico tries to hide is now showing again but only for a few seconds before he masks it. "I will take care of everything." Nico opens his laptop once again. "Why don't you rest before dinner? I will let you know when it's ready," he says while completely focused on his laptop screen.

I know what he is doing. I did that to for a long time during the first few months of my pregnancy. He is focusing on a trivial task rather than facing the problem.

I get up from the couch and head upstairs to the bedroom. Nothing I say will change anything right now. He knows the truth. He just needs to face it.

Chapter 42

NICO

I'm awoken to a noise. I grab my gun and look around in the dark room for an intruder but don't see anything. The clock on the stand says it's three in the morning.

I look down towards where Lily was lying sleeping but she's slumped over and grasping her bump. Alarm bells are going off in my head at her position.

"Lily? What's wrong?"

"Something's wrong." She stops talking when she leans forward in pain.

I jump out of bed and pull her into my arms and carry her out, not caring I'm only wearing a pair of sweatpants.

I see Carter jogging down the hallway. "What's wrong?"

"We need to get to the hospital now," I tell him as I continue my way downstairs towards the elevator. Carter is following behind me.

Lily's body is covered in a full sweat and the pain she is in is written all over her face.

She shudders before crying in pain. I wish I could take it all away from her. If I could take her place, I would in a heartbeat.

We get to the ground floor and Carter opens his truck back door. "I'll drive." I nod, getting into the back with Lily. She digs her nails into my shoulder as another round of pain goes through her.

"It's going to be okay. We will be at the hospital soon," I soothe into her hair. I don't know who I'm trying to comfort, her or me.

Carter gets us to the hospital and I carry Lily inside. The doctors and nurses examine her and then move her to a hospital room.

I want to strangle each one for being so slow. They take their time doing every little task.

Lily cries out in pain and I grasp her hand into mine. I give the nurse writing down Lily's vitals a death glare that causes her to stutter and say she will get the doctor right away.

For the doctor's sake he better get here soon, or he might find himself dead tomorrow morning.

Carter barges into the hospital room and throws a white t-shirt my way. "Has the doctor said anything?"

I pull the t-shirt over my head and pull it on. "No, those fuckers are useless. We should have called Dr. Watson."

"Nico," Lily moans quietly in pain.

I face her and tighten my grasp around her small delicate hand. Not hard enough to cause her pain but enough that she can feel me.

"What is it? Are you in pain?" I turn to Carter. "Do me a favor and drag the fucking doctor here will you?"

Carter heads towards the exit to get the damn doctor.

"Nico," Lily tries to speak through pained breathes. "It hurts so much."

I raise our joined hands and kiss her knuckles. "I know and I wish I could take it all away and carry the pain for you."

Lily's beautiful emerald eyes water. "I would never want you in pain."

"I've caused you so much pain already. I took everything from you, your family, your reputation, your life. It's all gone because of me."

Lily gives me a small smile despite her watery eyes. "Yet I don't regret any of it. I decided long time ago I would not have any regrets and I don't. I don't regret being with you, I don't regret loving you, I don't regret a single thing."

"You don't mean that."

"I do." Lily's smile grows. "I mean every single word."

Her words wash over me like a tidal wave. I don't deserve her. Lily clutches my hand and snaps her brows together as another round of pain hits her.

Fuck this, if I have to kill half the staff here to get them to make Lily priority, I will.

I hear the door bang open, and Carter walks in dragging a doctor by his neck. He lets the doctor go who looks around with terrified eyes.

"Carter, I don't think Nico meant you should literally drag a doctor here," Lily speaks with a pained edge.

Little does my sweet Lily know, I did. I would have been okay if Carter brought in a doctor with a bullet hole in him as long as he is still able to help Lily.

Carter shrugs and pushes the doctor forward. "Go on, do your job."

The doctor looks around before slowly walking towards Lily's chart. After a few seconds of reading, I get impatient. "Well?" I bark.

The doctor flinches. "It seems your wife is labor." I don't miss the doctor calling Lily my wife. The word feels like a stab in my chest at what little I can offer Lily. I glance over to Lily and she is in too much pain to have noticed.

"I could have told you that," I respond with annoyance at the doctor stating the obvious. Not sure if anger rising through me is from him calling Lily my wife, or little they are doing to help her. Mostly likely both. "Do something. She's in pain."

The doctor clears his throat. "There isn't much we can do. She is only 6 centimeters dilated. She needs to be 10 centimetres in order to give birth. We can give her an epidural for the pain in the meantime."

"Then give it to her." I glare the doctor. They have left her in pain for the last hour when they could have given her something a long time ago. I push away the urge to smash the doctor's head open to see how long he lasts without any pain medication.

My thoughts of breaking the doctor's skull open are interrupted by Lily's sweet voice. "How long before I will reach 10 centimeters?"

The doctor looks at Lily as he answers, "It can take anywhere from an hour to a few days."

"What the fuck did you just say? A few days!" I snap at the doctor.

The doctor whips his head in my direction. "I-it could be a few hours. It's hard to say." I don't miss the doctor slowly backing up towards the exit. His attempt to run is hindered when his back collides with Carter. He turns slowly to Carter who scowls at the doctor. "I was just going to get the epidural to help with the pain."

"I'll come with you," Carter states.

The doctor swallows a number of times before putting his head down in defeat. "Okay, follow me." The doctor exits and Carter follows him out.

I turn back to Lily and kiss the top of her head. "You're going to be okay."

She sweetly smiles. "I already knew that."

Chapter 43

NICO

The doctor returned a few minutes later with Carter in tow to give Lily an epidural to help with the pain. I could tell it made a difference right away; since getting the shot she seemed to be on some sort of a high.

For a while she was speaking nonsense but as long as she wasn't in pain, I was happy. I could listen to her speak gibberish all day long.

At around eight in the morning she was fully dilated to give birth.

I wanted to shoot the doctor for having a full view of Lily's cervix and I know that I'm being ridiculous, but I don't like the idea of anyone seeing Lily's parts besides me. Doctor or not.

I considered killing him anyways for leaving Lily in pain for so long, but my plans are put on pause when it was time for Lily to push.

She screamed in so much pain that her face went a shade of beet red I've never seen on her.

I felt utterly useless in that moment. I wanted to make the pain stop but there was nothing I could do. She clutched my hand for dear life as she pushed through each pain.

After a number of agonising screams from Lily she slumped back into the hospital bed and the room went silent.

Then the room was filled with a high-pitched cry from the baby.

The doctor hands Lily our baby boy who is covered in grime but still the most adorable thing I've ever seen.

He is pressed against Lily's chest as she looks down at him. Her face is glistening with sweat, yet she is still the most beautiful woman in the room.

The nurse walks over to us. "We need to take him to clean him up and do some tests." She looks up at me. "You can come with us while we do the tests."

Lily looks up at me. "Go with them and make sure he is safe."

I lean down and give Lily a gentle kiss. "I'll be right back."

The nurse takes our son and cleans him up. Without the grime, he looks even cuter. He is my son after all, of course he would have inherited my genes.

After a series of tests to make sure he is perfect health, I take him back to Lily's room.

I enter her hospital room and find Carter sitting next to Lily's bed. Lily is passed out asleep.

Carter rises from his seat. "So how is he?"

"He is just perfect." I look up at Carter. "How is Lily?"

"Tired. The doctor said it's normal after giving birth for her to be exhausted. I called Alessio and let him know. He and Anna want to come by and visit. I hope that's okay."

"Yeah of course." I would have called Alessio myself, but I was too preoccupied with everything else.

"Can I hold him?" Carter asks.

I hand Carter my son who holds him in his arms. We both have had practice holding Alessio's kids, so we know where to support the baby.

The baby squints open his eyes.

VENGEFUL PRINCE

Carter looks down at his eyes. "Do I see a hint of green in his eyes?"

Usually, a baby's eye color is not visible until they are a few months old, but our son is already showing a slight green in his eyes. The same as his mother. "I noticed that too earlier."

"Have the both of you decided on a name?"

"No, not yet."

A knock is heard at the door before Alessio opens it and walks in. Behind him is Anna and Emma.

Not being able to hold in the happiness anymore, I announce, "I have a son!"

Alessio and Anna smile at my reaction. They both offer congratulations and give me hugs before taking turns holding the baby. Lily is still completely out so they decide to come back later when she is awake and more prepared for guests.

As they are about to leave, I notice Emma pouting with her hands crossed against her chest. I squat down in front of her. "What's wrong?"

"I wanted a sister. But now I have another *brother*." She turns around and faces Anna. "Mommy, can you have a sister?"

Anna freezes at Emma's question whereas Alessio chuckles. "I think our daughter wants a sister."

Anna nudges Alessio in the side. "Not happening." She smiles down at Emma. "I already have a beautiful daughter. You are all I need."

Emma turns to Carter. "Can you give me a sister?" Carter turns to stone at Emma's question. We all burst out laughing at Carter's reaction.

Alessio picks up Emma. "Come on, mia cara. Time to go home."

Alessio, Anna and Emma leave and Carter heads out soon after.

Having spent the night here with us, I'm sure he is exhausted.

Chapter 44

LILY

After spending a couple days at the hospital, we are finally being released.

Nico had informed me he has set up a crib in one of the other spare rooms at Carter's penthouse.

Anna has also stopped by every day with a catalog of baby things for me to pick stuff out of.

I just finished packing my bag and put the baby in his baby carrier when the nurse walks in. "We just need you to complete the birth certificate form and sign it and you can go." I grab hold of the clipboard with the form and pen from the nurse's hand and stare at the form. "You can drop it off in the front when you are done," she says before leaving.

I sit on the bed next to the carrier and try and figure out what I'm supposed to write.

I fill out most of the form but leave the father section and his last name blank. Nico and I decided on the name Gabriele for our son, but we hadn't discussed his last name.

Nico walks into the room. "Are you ready to go?" He walks over to the baby carrier and smiles down at Gabriele. He looks up at me and furrows his brows. "Lily?"

"We need to fill out his birth certificate. I don't know what to write." The form brings a wave of emotions I had been pushing down for a while. "He can't have your last name because he is illegitimate and he can't have mine since my family disowned me."

Nico grabs the clipboard out of my hand and starts to fill it out. I look over his shoulder and see he is writing Vitale for his last name.

"Nico, he can't have your last name." As much as it pains me but that is how it works in our world.

"He is my son and he will have my last name. I don't care who says otherwise."

I open my mouth to stop him, but he gives me a look over his shoulder that shuts me up. I hate when he does that.

After filling up the form he signs under the father section. "I'll go drop this off. I'll be right back." He leaves the room with the form.

I look at my son Gabriele, who is sound asleep in his carrier.

Despite Nico giving him his last name and acknowledging our son, he will never be accepted. Not as long as I am the other woman.

NICO

We get to the penthouse, and I carry Gabriele in his baby carrier upstairs. Lily insisted on doing it, but she is still very weak. I don't want her hurting herself.

Lily takes Gabriele out of his carrier and looks at the clock. "It's almost his feeding time."

"We set up Gabriele's room across from us. It has everything he should need. Anna made sure to order everything you liked from those catalogs she brought and some other things she thought you might need."

"Will you thank her for me? I did before but I want her to know how much I appreciate everything she has done."

I nod. "I will. Why don't you rest after you feed him? I'll watch over him."

She smiles at me tiredly. "Maybe I'll take a small nap after his feeding."

Lily has been up for days now taking care of Gabriele. I need to be back at work soon but I'm considering asking Alessio and Anna for Greta to help out for a short while.

I hear a ruckus downstairs. I can't make out the words or what is happening, but my guard is up.

Lily looks towards the door. "Is something wrong downstairs?" she takes a step towards the hallway but I stop her.

"Stay here. I'll go check it out. I'm sure it's nothing but you and Gabriele should stay up here."

I close the door behind me and pull out my gun just in case. It's impossible for an outsider to get up here but I don't want to risk it. Not with Lily and Gabriele up here.

I get downstairs and to my annoyance, I put away my gun.

Gia is trying to get past Carter who is blocking her from entering.

"What the fuck are you doing here?" I ask Gia.

She snarls at me, "I thought I should come by say congratulations to your whore for giving birth to a bastard."

I get in Gia's face. "Call them that again and watch what happens."

She startles for a second before giving me a smirk. "Everyone will be calling them that. After all, that is what they are. A whore and a bastard!"

I grab Gia by the neck whose eyes are about to bug out of her sockets. I push her back and throw her into the elevator. "Don't fucking come here again unless you want to die."

"You think you can stay here and play house with that whore? Think again, Nico. I am your wife, don't forget that."

VENGEFUL PRINCE

The elevators door closes shut, and I slam my fist into the steel doors.

Carter pats my shoulder. "Don't let her get into your head."

I turn around and face him. "She's right though. Lily and Gabriele will never be accepted. I can't take Lily to parties and events. My son will never be allowed in the organization."

"Fuck the parties, they were boring anyways. And I know Alessio would allow Gabriele in and would even make him an underboss."

"But it wouldn't matter. He will always be the bastard son. No one will follow him. They will look down on my son because of *my* actions."

Carter doesn't respond, I know he knows I am right. Alessio could give Gabriele any title he wants but no one will follow or respect him. Not as long as he has the title of bastard. Not only have I ruined Lily's life, but I've ruined my son's.

Chapter 45

LILY

    Nico told me to wait upstairs, and I should have but I needed to know what was happening. I listened to Gia call me a whore and our son a bastard. Despite Nico's refusal as first, he knows the truth.

    I head back into our bedroom, the room I am occupying with another woman's husband. Gabriele stirs in my arms, and I know he is hungry.

    I take a seat in the middle of the bed and feed my son.

    After feeding and burping him, I head towards the room across from us to put Gabriele in his crib.

    I switch on the light and find the entire room decorated. The walls are a light blue and there is a stuffed toy mountain in the corner of the room.

    My eyes stink with emotion. I kiss Gabriele on his soft cheek and put him in his new crib.

    He may not be accepted in our world but at least he will have everything he could need. He might be looked down by others, but he will be loved by his family.

I head back to my room and change into a pair of sleep shorts and shirt and try and get some sleep. Despite being mentally and physically tired, I can't fall asleep.

I walk over to my hospital bag and pull out the new phone Nico had got me.

There isn't anyone I would call, but Nico wanted me to call him if there was anything I needed even if he was at work. Anna also saved her number in there so we can text.

I dial a number I know by heart and hit call. It rings for a couple seconds before being picked up.

"Hello?" Enzo answers.

My throat tightens at hearing my brother's voice. "Enzo, it's me."

"You shouldn't have called. You can't call me anymore."

His words feel like lashes against my heart. "Don't say that."

"You left, Lily."

"You know why." My voice cracks and along with it, the emotions I had hid away from dealing with the pain. "Please Enzo. I don't know what to do."

"You want to come back home?" There is a slight hopefulness in his voice.

"I can't, you know that." Even if my papa didn't disown me, I don't think I could leave Nico again. It was hard the first time and since coming back, I know I belong with him. "I had my son. His name is Gabriele." Enzo doesn't say a word, so I keep going. "He is beautiful and perfect. But others don't see him like that. Others see him like you and our family did." Tears spring out of me as I confess my pain to my brother. "He doesn't deserve this. He deserves so much more."

"You deserved so much more. I will make sure you get it. I need you to believe in me and make me a promise. If you ever want to come home, you will call me. I will bring you back. Promise me that you will contact me if for any reason you want to come home."

"I wouldn't be accepted. Papa would never accept me."

"I don't care about Papa or anyone else. I will be taking over soon. Promise me, Lily."

"I promise."

"I have to go now but do me a favor and send me a picture of my nephew when you get the chance."

I smile. "Of course."

Enzo hangs up the call soon after and a weight that has been on my chest smothering me has been lifted. I might not be any more accepted in Chicago then I am here, but least I know I still have someone to turn to if I needed it. But I know it in my heart I won't.

Chapter 46

LILY

I push Gabriele in his stroller with Anna walking beside me as she pushes her son Daniele in his stroller.

It's been a few weeks since Gabriele has been born and it's nice being outside. I needed the change in scenery.

Behind us are two enormous guards following close behind. One is Anna's guard Dino who scowls at anything that moves and then there is my new guard, Mario.

Nico had said the guard was meant to protect us and growing up as a mafia princess I was used to it.

I don't know if Mario's job is to protect us from threats outside the organization or inside. I had heard Nico tell Mario no one but Alessio, Carter or Anna was allowed near me or Gabriele.

I suspect Nico might have been trying to keep Gia from me. But I will take her wrath any day. I deserve it after all.

We stop in front of a bench at the playground and Emma runs to the swings. We take a seat on the bench as we watch Emma swing.

"How have things been?" Anna asks.

"Good I guess considering the situation."

"Alessio told me your new place with Nico is almost ready. You can now have your own place."

I shrug. "I don't mind staying at Carter's. Plus, I know how close Nico is with his brothers. I worry he might miss them being so far away."

Anna laughs. "You guys will be five minutes drive away. Ten minutes to walk. You won't be that far."

I smile. "I guess you're right."

Daniele pulls on his stroller buckles and gets loose trying to climb out. Anna sighs. "What am I going to do with this one? He is growing up so fast and he tries to run every chance he gets." Anna pushes him back in the stroller and tries to lock the buckles around him, but he fidgets in her grasp.

She is finally able to get him back in after a few moments. Anna looks up and startles. "Where is Emma?" Her voice rises in panic. "Where is my daughter?" She stands from the bench and looks around in a frenzy.

"She's right there on the slides." I point Emma out for Anna.

Anna falls back onto the bench with her hand on her heart. It looked like she might have had a small heart attack there.

"Of course, she's right there," she says in relief.

I gently touch her hand. "Are you okay?"

Anna nods. "I just get scared whenever I don't see the kids. I know Alessio has increased security but after the thing with Ronan, I still get scared occasionally. I try not to but sometimes my mind goes back to the past."

Hearing Ronan's name sends a chill down my spine. Anna couldn't be possibly talking about the same Ronan I almost married.

"What thing with Ronan?" I ask, dreading the answer at the same time.

Anna looks at me. "You didn't know? I thought you knew." Her eyes widen and she grasps my hand into hers. "I'm so sorry Lily. I thought Nico told you."

"Told me what?" My voice sounding calm, but my mind is anything but calm.

"Ronan Fitzgerald kidnapped me and Emma while I was pregnant. It's the reason for the war between the Irish and Italians. It's why Nico…" Anna looks at me with pitying eyes. "I'm sorry Lily. I didn't know and when Alessio told me, it was after you were returned to your family. I'm to blame for everything that happened to you."

I take in Anna's words. Ronan kidnapped her and Emma. Ronan treated me like trash, and I was supposed to be his wife. I can't even imagine what he did to Anna and Emma.

"You're not to blame. Besides if Nico didn't come after me to get to Ronan, I wouldn't be here. I would be married to Ronan who was a psychopath. Things worked out for the best."

It did. It might have not all worked out, but it is for the better.

"I want you to know I am sorry," Anna apologizes again.

"You have nothing to be sorry for." I give her a smile, "I mean it. Things did work out for the best."

After our outing, we head back to the penthouse for the kids to rest. Anna and I agreed to have lunch in a few days. She had even suggested inviting some other wives of higher members within the organization, but I declined.

I know she was only trying to help me, but I wouldn't be accepted. The wives may not speak ill of me in front of Anna's face as she is the wife of the Capo but I'm sure they wouldn't have a problem saying it directly to me while her back is turned.

Besides, that is Gia's world and place. I have no spot in that circle.

NICO

I get back to the penthouse around 10pm. Carter is still out working and probably won't be home for a couple more hours.

I enter the living room and find the television on, but Lily is passed out on the couch. I pick her up in my arms and she stirs in her sleep from being moved.

I carry her upstairs to our bedroom and place her on the bed. I cover her with the blanket and kiss her on the forehead before closing the door behind me.

I head over to Gabriele's room and peek into his crib and find him wide awake. He smiles when he sees me. I pick him up and head to the kitchen.

It's around his feeding time and I don't want to wake up Lily.

Luckily there is a bottle of pumped milk already in the fridge. Lily had pumped some this morning for her outing with Anna today.

I'm glad Anna and Lily are becoming friends. I worried what the toll of having no one would do to Lily.

I warm the bottle of milk and feed Gabriele. He starts to fall asleep in my arms as he continues to drink. Once the bottle is empty and I'm sure he is asleep I pull the bottle away. Gabriele continues to make little sucking motions with his mouth a few more times before falling into a slumber.

He has my nose and chin but Lily's eyes. They're not prominent yet but each day the green becomes brighter.

I rub my finger against his soft downy hair and can't help but smile. I might not be able to give him what he deserves today but one day I will make sure he and his mother have everything they deserve.

Chapter 47

LILY

Nico has been working late for the last couple of days. I haven't had the chance to see him but today the doctor gave me the all clear for us to be intimate again. I need that. I need to feel that bond we had together.

Since I've returned from Chicago, Nico has treated me like some fragile glass doll.

Well not tonight.

I just finished feeding Gabriele and put him to sleep. Now I just need to wait for Nico to get back home.

It's almost 11pm when I hear the door to our bedroom open. As soon as I see him walk in, I can't take it anymore.

I jump off the bed and clash into Nico's hard body. I wrap my arms around his neck and kiss him.

He laughs against my lips before pulling away. "Excited to see me?"

"More than excited." I take a step back and untie my robe and toss it to the side, leaving me completely naked.

I have some stretch marks from my pregnancy, but I hope Nico doesn't mind.

Nico's eyes dilate. "Lily, the doctor said we're not supposed to…"

"He gave me the go ahead today," I cut him off.

And that is all I needed to say because Nico is on me all of a sudden. He wraps his hands around my waist and collides his lips to mine while pushing me back towards the bed.

My knees hit the mattress and I fall back with Nico on top of me. He takes off his jacket and shirt and I help him by unbuckling his belt. He tosses his clothes to the side and pushes me further on to the bed.

I feel his cock on my thigh and a warmth between my legs takes over.

I need him inside me now. Nico nudges his tip into my opening and I feel like I'm going to come apart already. He slowly fills me up and I shudder at the fullness.

"Tell me if it's too much," Nico says. But I'm not listening. I just need him to move.

I wiggle underneath him until he finally moves. First, he goes slow and then with each thrust, he speeds up.

I shift which causes him to hit deeper. He speeds up even more and I can feel myself getting to where I want to be. I just need a little more. I wrap my legs around Nico and the new position causes me to moan as he hits deeper. Then the blinding stars finally hit me. Nico follows soon after and releases inside me while pulsating.

We are both out of breath and sweaty when we fall against the mattress.

Nico leans down and kisses me, and I soften into his touch. "You know I love you."

I place my hands on Nico's cheeks. "I know, and I love you."

Chapter 48

LILY

I'm at the grocery store in the vegetable area grabbing produce for dinner tonight. Since arriving to New York, Nico has either made dinner or I've ordered in.

I thought it would be nice for me to do the cooking for once. I grab some green peppers and place it in my cart.

I take my time looking around since Anna was kind enough to watch Gabriele for me while I did some shopping. Usually, I can't get much done with an infant baby with me.

I'm about to round the corner with my cart when I stop in my tracks.

"Hello Lily," Ronan says as he walks towards me.

I take a step back and look behind me for Mario. He has two men standing beside him. Irish men.

"He can't help you. He seems to be pre-occupied by my men." Ronan puts an arm around me. "When I heard you were back in town I was quite surprised. Then I found out you had the Vitale bastard's child. Tell me Lily, how did that happen?"

"I-I…" I stutter.

Ronan raises his hand. I think he is going to hit me, so I flinch back, but instead he pushes my hair behind my ear.

"Don't bother lying to me. A little birdie told me you were having an affair with Nico Vitale while we were engaged." Ronan pushes me forward. "Don't make a scene, Lily, I would hate to have to kill your guard and everyone in here."

I would like to believe he is lying. He wouldn't be stupid enough to go on a killing spree with dozens of eyewitnesses and cameras around. But this is Ronan.

I force my feet to walk forward.

"Good girl, if only you were this good while we were engaged."

I walk out of the store with Ronan and he pushes me towards a black SUV. I look back at Mario and one of the two men knock him unconscious with the butt of their gun. A few people scream at the sight of a gun and run in fear.

I turn on my feet and try and make a run for but only make it a few steps before Ronan grabs me by the hair and pulls me into the SUV.

The door slams shut behind me and I go for the door handle, but I'm knocked out by a punch to the face.

Chapter 49

LILY

My head hurts as if I hit it on something hard. Or someone hit me hard.

I push up into a sitting position and look around me. I'm on a roof of a building. It's night now and I can hear cars honking but no people. This place seems familiar, but I can't figure out where I am.

I get on my feet and see a door on the other side of the roof. I walk towards it, but I'm blocked when Ronan steps in front of me.

"Going somewhere?" He gives me an unnerving smile.

I take a few steps back. "Ronan, I can explain." My back collides with Carlo, who pushes me forward towards Ronan.

"Explain? Explain to me how my soon to be wife was whoring herself out to the enemy?"

I trip over something and fall on to my back. I try to get up, but Ronan kicks me in the ribs. I wheeze at the impact.

"Explain to me, Lily, how you were able to betray me and have the enemy's bastard." Another kick to the rib follows. "Explain to me why you're such a whore." This time he kicks me so hard blood splatters out from my mouth.

"Ronan please," I beg.

He grabs me by the hair and pulls me up. "I can't believe I almost married a pathetic whore."

"That's what she is, a whore." I look towards the voice and to my shock find Gia standing behind Ronan. She looks at me with smug smile. "I'm going to enjoy killing you. Then I'm going to get back with my husband after I drown your little spawn."

I push and kick Ronan away to get to Gia. "Don't you dare touch my son!"

Ronan throws me to the ground. "She is all yours." He takes out his gun and hands it to Gia.

"Gia, don't do this. I never intended to hurt you. I didn't even know about you," I try and reason with Gia.

"But you did eventually, and you still whored yourself out to my husband. Gave him everything I should have!" Gia steps in front of me. "Any last words before I finish you off?"

I get on my knees as tears stream down my face. "I'm to blame. Kill me but leave my son alone. Send him back to Chicago to my brother Enzo but just don't hurt him."

Gia aims the gun to my forehead and I close my eyes knowing what's to come. I pray Gabriele makes it to Enzo. He will take care of him. I know my brother will.

Then a silent whistle is heard through the air. I open my eyes and find Gia on the ground bleeding from her heart with the gun laying in front of her.

Carlo takes out his gun. Another round is heard as Ronan ducks behind a ventilator on the roof. Carlo falls to the ground with a bullet hole to his heart.

I quickly grab the gun from the ground and run towards the door. Ronan chases after me as I pull the door open but I don't look back. I'm running down the stairs when Ronan collides into me causing us to fall down the stairs.

The gun flies out of my hand and a shot fires as it hits the wall before the gun lands a few steps down. I crawl towards the gun, but Ronan grabs my leg and drags me back.

Ronan is now on top of me and begins to choke me. "You stupid bitch!" He slams my head against the floor hard and I start to black out from the lack of oxygen and blinding pain. I see a shadow come from behind Ronan and then everything goes dark.

Chapter 50

NICO

When I was informed Ronan had kidnapped Lily, I lost it. I wanted to kill Mario for failing at protecting Lily and then I wanted to go into the Irish territory and kill everyone of those fuckers before I finished off their boss.

But first I needed to find Lily.

When Mario had mentioned he thought he saw Gia get into Ronan's car before being knocked out, I knew right then the little bitch had something to do with this.

I tracked her phone and found out she was at Lily's old apartment that I first saw her at.

Of course, it must have been Ronan's idea; the fucker gets his kicks playing games. Taking Lily back to where I first met her and where it all started must have been another one of those games.

When we barged into the empty apartment, I was sure we made a mistake. Then we heard a shot from the roof.

When I got almost to the top and saw my Lily being strangled by that fucker Ronan, I saw red. I wanted to put a bullet through his head and kill him. But that would be too easy for that fucker. He deserved so much more. So, I let the little fucker live for now.

Carter took him back to Encore to be locked away in one of our underground cells, while I took Lily home.

Dr. Watson checked her out and advised she will be fine but has a broken rib. She will probably have a mild headache from the blows to the head and will need lots of rest.

I kissed Lily and left her in the care of Anna's hands as I went back to Encore. There is too much anger inside me and I needed to release it.

I get to Encore and head straight to the basement. Alessio and Carter have already started.

Ronan is tied to a chair naked with cuts and bruises all over him. When I walk into the cement room, Ronan looks up at me and smiles. "I was able to get my hands on at least 2 out of 3 Vitale men's women." He turns to Carter. "Too bad you don't have someone or I could had some fun with her as well."

Carter punches Ronan and a bone cracking noise can be heard.

Ronan spits blood on to the ground. "Fuck you. When my brother gets out of prison, he will finish off what I started."

Alessio picks up a knife from the table on the side. "And we will skin him the same we are going to skin you."

"Then there is my nephew. You will never be rid of us. We will finish you off."

Alessio walks over to Ronan. "But we will be rid of you."

Ronan squirms in his chair as Alessio pierces his skin. Carter and I hold him still as Alessio cuts him up.

Ronan's agonising screams are music to my ears. After everything he has done to Lily, Anna and Emma. He deserves everything we will give him.

Ronan is a bloody mess on the ground. We consider killing him off but decide for round two in the morning. The fucker doesn't get to die that easily.

I lock Ronan's cell door behind me. Mario comes running down the hallway. "We found Gia and Carlos dead on the rooftop."

"How did Gia die?" Alessio asks.

"Maybe Ronan killed her. She thought she could betray us and help him but after Ronan got what he wanted, he killed her," I suggest.

"We could ask him once he wakes up tomorrow morning," Carter proposes.

Mario shakes his head. "No Gia was killed by a sniper. We found evidence there was someone across the building. They shot Gia and Carlo in the heart."

In the heart. There is only one sniper in the entire world who chooses to kill by aiming for a person's heart. Most snipers kill by aiming for the head, as it the most effective and efficient way to kill.

Aiming for the heart requires a lot of skill and is difficult. If the hit is the slightest bit off, the person can survive. Whereas a hit to the head is instant death.

From my brothers' faces they are thinking the same thing.

Marco Esposito from the Mancini family killed Gia and Carlo and saved Lily.

LILY

I open my eyes and see the familiar ceiling. I get into a sitting position and look around. My side aches with a horrible pain.

I'm lack in the penthouse in our bedroom.

I jump out of bed and run to Gabriele's room. He is not in his crib. I run downstairs and find Anna sitting on the couch with Gabriele in her arms.

"You're up." Anna pushes to her feet and walks over to me. "How are you feeling?"

"I have a pounding headache and pain on my side but aside from that, fine." I pick my son up and kiss his head. I thought I wasn't going to see him ever again. I look at Anna for answers. "What happened? How did I get here?"

"Alessio, Nico, and Carter tracked Gia's phone and found you. I can't believe Gia was working with Ronan." Anna shakes her head in disappointment.

"What happened to Ronan?"

"He was taken back to Encore. As far as I'm aware of he is alive, but I doubt he will stay that way for long. If Alessio or Nico don't kill him, my brothers will. They've been wanting to get their hands on him since he kidnapped me but out of respect for Alessio, they let him deal with Ronan."

I've heard rumors of the Petrov family, and none have been good. They don't show mercy or kindness to anyone.

I heard the Petrov brothers even killed their own father and took over the family business. I don't see them as the caring type, but Anna speaks about them with such love.

"I already fed Gabriele and he is falling asleep. Why don't you rest?" Anna recommends.

Rest would be nice right now with the pounding headache but I need to be with my son right now. "I'm fine. I think I rather be with Gabriele right now."

"I understand. I'll be one call away if you need me." Anna gives me a hug which causes Gabriele to fuss in my arms but not enough to wake him. "Call me for anything and anytime."

I thank Anna for everything she has done before she heads up to her floor to be with her family.

I sit on the couch and memorise each piece of hair on Gabriele's head.

When I had closed my eyes and waited for death, all I could see was Nico and Gabriele. They were the last thing I wanted to see before I died.

The elevator doors open, and Carter and Nico walk out. They are drenched in blood.

I scrunch my nose at them. "I really hope that isn't either of your blood."

Carter smiles. "No and I'm going to sleep like a baby tonight." He heads upstairs and I look for Nico for more information.

"It's Ronan's blood."

"Is he dead?" I know I should be more concerned with the amount of blood on them but the thought that Ronan can get to me scares me more than anything else.

"Not yet." Nico comes to sit beside me on the couch. "He doesn't get to die so easily. But we will finish him off in a couple days."

"Is that why Carter's so happy? You finally got Ronan."

"No, Carter gets excited anytime he gets to torture someone, it's just a bonus it's Ronan."

A tremor goes down my spine. I forget sometimes who Carter is and what he does for a living. He is the Vitale enforcer for a reason.

Nico looks at me and gently traces a bump forming on the side of my head. "He is going to pay for this and everything he has done."

"I can't believe my papa had wanted me to marry Ronan. I would have never survived."

"I wouldn't have survived without you."

I smile at Nico. "So I guess it's a good thing you came into my life."

Nico smirks. "Still seeing the good in the bad I did."

I lean over and kiss Nico with one hand cupping his jaw. He deepens the kiss and I moan against his lips. I place my forehead against

Nico's. "There is no bad." I give him another kiss before I pull away when I feel Gabriele stir in my arms.

In the past I may have regretted my actions and the choices I made when I found out who Nico was but now here in this moment, I have no regrets. I would do it all again to be here.

Chapter 51

LILY

It's been a week since Ronan grabbed me from the grocery store. Nico had told me last night Ronan was officially dead. After a week of torture, they finally killed him. I know I should feel guilt for what Nico and his brothers did but I don't.

Anna had told me the full story of what Ronan had done to her, and despite her claiming she is fine now, I can still see the side effects from what Ronan did on her.

Nico had also mentioned he suspected my family had something to do with Gia's death.

I had called Enzo but he refused to speak to me about business. He had previously said he planned to make things right and give me everything I deserved but I didn't think he meant killing Nico's wife.

As much as I hated what Gia did, I can't help but blame myself for her death. Anna had mentioned Gia was always like this but that doesn't excuse the pain I caused her.

I'm strolling through the park with Gabriele in his stroller and

Mario following close behind.

Nico wanted to kill him for failing to protect me but I had pointed out he was outnumbered and if he did try anything the Irish would have killed him. Then he would never have been able to tell him about Gia, thus allowing them to track me down.

Nico had agreed to give Mario another chance but made it clear to him if I so much as got a scratch on me he would pay with his life.

I didn't take Nico's words to be literal, but Mario clearly did. He almost had a stroke when he saw me come downstairs in heels.

When I refused to change out of my heels, I heard him do a silent prayer I don't trip and scratch myself accidently.

I'm meeting Nico here for lunch. It will be our first outing in months. Which is why I made the extra effort to dress nice today.

We walk by a dog park and the cutest little dog comes running towards me. I squat down. "Hi there." I pet the dog, who wiggles his tail in excitement.

The dog owner comes running towards me. "I'm so sorry. He has a habit of… wow." The owner makes eye contact with me. "Sorry, I was thrown off by your beauty."

My cheeks go red at his compliment. I straighten and he follows my lead.

The owner sticks out his hand. "Hi, my name is Dan."

I shake his hand. "Hi, I'm Lily."

Dan flips my hand in his. "No wedding ring, so I take it you're single?" I purse my lips as I try and figure out what me and Nico are.

As I'm contemplating what to tell Dan, a hand wraps around me and I'm pulled back and collide into a strong body.

"She is not fucking single," Nico rages from behind me.

Dan scratches his head. "Sorry man, I didn't see a ring on her finger and just assumed."

"Well, you assumed wrong. Now fuck off before I break your hand."

Dan gives me a smile before walking away. Nico growls behind me and moves to follow Dan. I spin around and kiss Nico before he murders a man in the park in daylight.

I can feel the anger disappearing from Nico at the feel of our lips. I pull away. "We should get going, I'm hungry."

Nico narrows his eyes at me. "I know what you did there."

I shrug. "I don't know what you mean," I say, playing oblivious.

I start to push the stroller away when Mario leans forward. "If I ever piss off Nico, make sure to be there."

"Mario! What the fucking are you saying to Lily?" Nico snaps.

"Nothing boss, just how that dog owner was one ugly fucker," Mario says with a big smile.

Nico nods. "I agree. He was ugly, wasn't he?"

"Yeah, he was, boss."

I roll my eyes. "Can we please go eat? I'm starving." Gabriele begins to get fussy in his stroller from being strapped in.

Nico unstraps Gabriele and holds him in my arms as we walk towards a small bistro near the park.

Luckily, we were able to get a table outside, perfect for a bright sunny day.

I'm going over the menu when the waiter walks up. "Are you guys ready to order?"

Nico orders first while I continue to look over the menu.

"I'll get a simple Caesar salad with water to drink," I order.

Despite not gaining a lot of weight during the pregnancy, I would like to lose the few pounds I did gain.

The waiter smiles. "Are you sure you don't want anything else?"

I nod. "Yes, I'm sure." I hand the menu to the waiter to take. He grabs the menu out of my hand and then takes the one lying in front of Nico.

"I'll be right back with your order." The waiter winks at me before walking away.

Nico narrows his eyes at the waiter's retreating back. "I should shoot him in the head."

"For what?" I turn back towards the waiter trying to figure out what I missed.

"He winked at you."

"He was just being friendly."

"He was hitting on you with me right here."

"While it's nice to know I have options," I joke. I don't care for the waiter and for some reason I don't see any other man but Nico. They all seem irrelevant since he came into my life.

Nico's jaw ticks. "Is that so?"

I shrug and look out across the street at the park. Not only it is a beautiful day to be out, but it also feels peaceful.

After everything, I'm okay and happy. I don't need anything else. As long as I'm with Nico and have Gabriele, I will be fine.

The waiter returns with our food and Nico glares at him with a look that suggests he may actually kill him.

Halfway through my lunch, Gabriele started to get fussy so we decided to leave which from Nico's continued glares at the waiter was probably for the best.

NICO

Lily just fed and put Gabriele to sleep in his crib. She is now balled up on the couch watching one of her reality shows. I go to sit beside her and wrap my arms around her. She molds into my side and continues to watch her show.

"The preview last week showed a fight between those two." Lily points to the screen with her remote.

I smirk at her watching the show with such intensity. "For someone who doesn't like boxing, you seem to be very excited over a fight on some reality show."

Lily rolls her eyes. "Well it's not really a fight. More like two grown women acting like children by throwing glasses of water at each other."

One of the women on the show reminds me of Gia with all the plastic surgery. Her funeral was a few days ago. As her husband, I had to attend but left as soon as it was over. I had no interest in sticking around for people to give me condolences. I didn't care for the bitch when she was alive and sure as hell don't now that she is dead. If the Mancini family didn't kill her, I would have for hurting Lily.

Her mother was bawling her eyes out throughout the service but her father and brother kept their heads hung.

Considering Gia betrayed the family by helping the Irish, she is considered a traitor and her funeral was kept small and simple.

Word had also spread that the Mancinis sent their enforcer to kill Gia out of retaliation for Lily. Rumors vary from Lily being kept prisoner by my family to being mentally broken from our torture. I hate every single rumor about Lily, but I rather be the monster in the story and she the victim than have people know the truth.

They wouldn't understand. They would call her names and shame her and she doesn't deserve any of that.

I grab Lily's small soft left hand into mine. I rub the area around the ring finger. The fucker at the park thought she was single because she didn't have a ring.

I've wanted to make Lily my wife and put a ring on her finger since the beginning for everyone to know she is mine. Due to my marriage to Gia, I wasn't able to before.

"We should get married," I say while looking at the missing ring on Lily's hand. I should get her the most beautiful diamond to match her.

Lily goes rigid. "That's not funny." She slides her hand out mine.

"I wasn't joking. Gia is dead so we can now get married."

"No, we can't."

"Why not?"

Lily turns off her show with the remote and faces me. "Gia just died a week ago. She was killed by my family. Her funeral was only two days ago. It wouldn't be right for us to get married."

"If not now, let's get married next month."

"That's not what I mean!" Lily moves to get up and I wrap my arm around her waist and pull her into my lap.

The smell of her strawberry shampoo is intoxicating. I try and focus on the matter on hand. "First of all, Gia would have been killed regardless because she betrayed the family. She is considered a traitor by all. Second I don't care if it is right or not. I want to marry you. I want you as my wife. Third you don't get a say. I've already decided and you can say no all you want but I will marry you."

"Nico…"

"I think next month on June 26 would be the perfect date to get married."

Lily turns in my grasp and furrows her eyebrows. "Why that date?"

"That's the day you came to New York City and I saw you for the first time."

Lily slowly smiles. "You remember the exact date."

"Of course, I do. It's the day my life changed forever. Marry me, Lily, and be my wife."

Lily bites on her lower lip before answering quietly with a smile, "Okay."

That is all I needed to hear. I kiss Lily and pull her closer to me. I can feel the smile on her lips.

"I won't ever let you regret us."

Her lips hover over mine as she breathes, "I know."

Chapter 52

LILY

It is my wedding day. I did my hair and makeup simple and wore a modest white dress. Nothing fancy or glamourous.

Despite Nico being the Vitale Family right hand man to the Capo, we decided to keep the wedding small. Only Nico's family was invited and no one else.

My heart ached at the thought of my family not being here, but I knew my parents would never come or accept this marriage. To them Nico kidnapped and took away their daughter.

I had called my papa and tried to explain the truth, but he huffed on the phone, "Did that bastard tell you to say these lies?" before telling me to never call again. I had made my choice and it was one I will live with.

I had at least hoped Enzo would come but he too doesn't see the truth. He wished me well over the phone but then said it would be best if we limited our contact. His words sliced me more than anything my parents could have said or done. From them I had expected it but not from Enzo.

Anna walks into the bridal room. "Are you ready?" She looks beautiful in her baby blue dress. Emma walks in behind her, in a matching colored dress with a flower crown in her hair and a basket of flowers.

"I'm ready." I rise from my chair and walk towards the door. We walk towards the church doors and Anna hands me my bouquet of flowers before rushing inside to let everyone know.

The wedding music begins, and the doors open. Emma walks ahead, throwing uncoordinated balls of flowers in every direction. Then I see Nico standing at the end looking utterly handsome in his tux and my heart skips a beat in excitement.

This is right. I feel it in my heart and soul.

NICO

Lily is officially my wife. The ceremony was small and simple but that is all I needed. We did a small party at Alessio's to introduce Lily to the other underbosses and higher up families.

They all feigned happiness for us, but I could tell by Lily's shaking hands she was afraid when each guest came up to congratulate us.

She worries she won't be accepted or doesn't belong. But she is wrong. Lily belongs next to me. That is her place. Anyone who says otherwise I will cut out their tongues.

But due to the ridiculous rumors, most believe I forced Lily into the marriage to legitimatize my son after I impregnated her by kidnapping and torturing her.

Another one of the underbosses' walks up with his wife to congratulate us.

His wife looks at Lily before shaking her head and saying under her breath, "Poor thing."

Lily strains to smile as they walk away. She leans into me. "What was that about?"

I shrug. "Who knows?"

Lily doesn't need to know about the rumors. Knowing Lily she would feel bad I'm considered a monster and would tell everyone the truth. Which would only bring her pain. I don't want to see her in pain ever. Besides I was known to be a monster by many before I met Lily, a few more stupid rumors won't do anything.

Gabriele screams in Carter's arms from across the room. Lily walks over to them and grabs hold of Gabriele. She cradles him against her chest, and he slowly stops crying.

Even from across the room, Lily's emerald wedding ring can be visibly seen on her hand.

The sales associate at the shop had tried to convince me to get a princess cut diamond for Lily, stating all women loved that style. But Lily isn't like other women. She doesn't care for superficial things like that.

I doubt she would have cared if I got her a simple gold band. But I needed everyone to know she is my wife. Mine.

I walk over to Lily and pull her back into my embrace. She looks up at me with a smile as Gabriele gives his own version of a drooled smile in her arms.

I kiss the side of her head. "I love you, Lily."

Lily smiles wider. "I love you too."

My wife and son. I don't need anything else.

Printed in Great Britain
by Amazon